Karma: Two to The Right

by Jermaine Hall

© Copyright 2018 by Jermaine Hall

Published by Semaj Publishing

Edited by Jermaine Hall and Raul Garcia

Cover Design: Sayana Designs

ISBN: 978-0998110349

Library of Congress: 2018938552

This book is available at a special discount for churches, schools and other educational institutions.

Contact Semaj Publishing
Author Bookings and Management
semajpub@hotmail.com

This book is dedicated to my 14 loving kids; Tracy, Tiffany, Jernay, Linda, (Josh) Jermaine Jr., Gerrod, Jayvorn, Jayquarn, Tanoya, Jared, Nazi,Toya, Marissia and Janiyah.

Table of Contents

The Game

In the locker room of the gymnasium as the boys are preparing to play the biggest game of their life. The lights are dim due to the many blown light bulbs but that doesn't affect the group of teenage boys. There is laughter as the boys are getting dressed in their basketball uniforms. Some are adjusting their uniforms to make sure that it is properly draped just in case someone takes a picture of them.

There is a loud deep voice that comes from the rear of the locker room. "Come on boys, let's get in a huddle for a team prayer," said Coach Brown, who is the deacon of the church. The boys dressed in there black and yellow uniforms bow their heads in anticipation of what coach would say. Coach extends his hands as he prays over the nine boys on the team for them to play their hearts out and win the championship game.

After the prayer, Coach turns to two of the boys and says, "Look boys, I know you got us this far and we're going to need you two out there on your 'A' game today."

"It's ok Coach; this is Jayvorn and Jayrode you're talking to. You know, two to the right," Jayvorn tells the coach all excited.

"Yeah coach, you know how we do. This game is going to be a breeze and I'll still make my appointment," Jayrode says.

"Ok boys, you know I am counting on all of

you out there on the court," the coach tells all the boys as he put his hand out for a team cheer and all the boys put their hands on top of his.

"On one! Two to the right!" Jayvorn says to the team.

"Two to the right!" they all yell as they turned and ran out of the locker room and down the hallway. The players were happy and yelled as they came into the gymnasium.

As they are running down the hallway, Jayvorn grabs Jayrode's arm just before they enter the gymnasium; the rest of the team has already gone in. "Yo, Jayrode, what you mean your appointment?"

"Look man, don't worry about it, because by the time I leave, we'll be up by 50 points over these bums!" Jayrode answers as he runs out into the gymnasium.

"Come on Jayvorn it's our time to shine now," Jayrode yells back too Jayvorn as he goes out to the gymnasium.

Jayrode and Jayvorn enter the gym. The crowd grows loud. They look around and you can tell how they felt by the look on their faces and their smile. It was if they made it to the NBA. Once Jayvorn hears the cheers he forgets all about Jayrode's appointment. He smiles and joins his teammates on the sideline as they watch the other team enter the gym in their blue and white uniforms.

The whole team hit the court and started to warm up. All the boys were looking good. Both teams grab some basketballs; start shooting around and warming up. Some players are stretching, shooting jump shots, and some are practicing their lay-ups.

Not long after the warm-up began it was time for the game as the coaches called their teams back to their benches. After a few minutes, the referee blows a whistle and walks over to the score table and asks for the game ball. The ref went out to the center of the court with the game ball. Both teams said their cheer and five boys from both sides went out to the court. The jump ball was thrown up and the game begins.

Jayrode explodes in the beginning, scoring the first 10 points. Jayvorn follows suit with 8. Near the end of the second quarter, the score was 38 to 20, they were up.

A few minutes later it was halftime. Jayrode is the first to the sideline. He looks at the time clock and says, "Coach, I got to go do something important. I be right back."

Coach Brown with a puzzled look on his face responds, "What do you mean?"

The rest of the players have reached the sideline. They are all drying themselves off and drinking water. They notice Jayrode talking to Coach.

"Look Coach, it's very important and I can't put it off," Jayrode answers him.

"Look Jayrode; we're in the middle of a game. Not only that, it's the championship game!" the Coach says loudly. The team hears him yelling and looks at the two talking.

"I know, but this can't wait and besides Coach, we're up by 18 points," Jayrode tells him.

"What is it that you *have* to leave right now?" the Coach is starting to get really annoyed.

"It's something for my mom it will only take a few minutes," Jayrode says with a serious look on his face.

"If it's only for a few minutes, why can't it wait until after the game?"

"Look Coach, I'm sorry, but I really got to go. I be right back!", Jayrode said with a look as if it really couldn't wait.

"Look boy! Do you want to play on this team or not? Because I'm not going to have you running off whenever you want and just come back. You're good, but no one person is a star on this team!", the coach tells him as he looks him seriously in his eyes.

Jayrode with a sad almost an apologetic look says, "I know Coach, and I do want to play but..."

"Look Coach, it's ok, we got it, let him go. He did say he be right back.", Jayvorn told the coach as he interrupted Jayrode.

"Ok boy, how long are you going to be?", the coach asks as if he didn't want Jayrode to go.

"A few minutes Coach," with excitement and relief in his voice Jayrode answers him.

"You're lucky you have friends who care and love you. Make it fast and be right back," says Coach with a serious look.

"I will Coach, thanks. I promise I be right

back", Jayrode tells him as he started running out of the gymnasium

As Jayrode is about to leave, Jayvorn pulls him aside. "Yo, Jayrode, what's up?", asking with a worried look on his face.

"Look man, it's nothing! If you let me go now, I will be right back," Jayrode tells him with a smirk on his face as if he was up to something.

"Ok man, even though we're up, we still need you out there!"

"Look man, we got this game in the bag. I know you're going to score another 20 points on them. For real man, I be right back, I promise.", Jayrode said pointing at the other team as if they were bums.

"Ok man, just hurry back," Jayvorn told him, as Jayrode goes to the sideline and grabs his duffle bag and ran out of the gym. On his way out the door, he bumped into a white man and almost knocked him down. "Excuse me! Jayrode yells back to the man as he kept going.

"Oh man, people need to learn how to slow down sometimes," the man said softly to himself as he went into the gym and took a seat in the upper bleachers. By that time the referee blows his whistle to start the second half of the game.

"Where is that boy now, the game is about to start," the coach said as they were in the huddle.

"Chill out coach! He just left," Jayvorn said with a smile on his face.

"Well, he just needs to be back!" the coach says with a smirk.

The second half of the game starts; Jayvorn and four of his teammates went back onto the floor. Jayvorn explodes in the second half of the game as they took the lead with his famous move, two to the right. Jayvorn scored 14 points and 6 assists by the middle of the second half. Jayvorn calls for a timeout by the time they go back on the court to finish up the second half Jayrode comes back. The score is 67 to 32. They are winning. Jayrode runs to the Coach and asks, "Hey coach, can I get back in the game now?", all excited.

"Hold on and have a seat. Like your teammates said, they got it!" the Coach answers him. He calls out to the boys on the floor. Jayrode sits on the bench with a look of betrayal on his face for not being able to get right back into the game. The referee blows his whistle again for the other team to take a timeout.

"You made it back in time, Jayrode!" Jayvorn says looking at the coach in a manner to say he told him he would be back.

"What's up Coach, are you going to put Jayrode back in the game?" Jayvorn asks.

"Yeah, are you Coach?" The other boys ask as they are all excited.

"Not right now boys. We are up and besides Jayrode needs to learn what's important. He can't just run out on his team in the middle of the game," the coach explains.

"But Coach," they all say.

"No buts! Let's go out there and finish this one!" Coach Brown says looking sternly at his team.

"Don't sweat it Jayrode, we'll win this one for you!" Jayvorn says to him.

"Win it for me! Come on, the game's already won. Look at that score. I don't know why they're going back out there," Jayrode says as he is pointing to the scoreboard.

"You know what, you're funny. But you're right. So just chill, you know how the Coach can be," Jayvorn says.

"Yeah, I know. I'm not sweating it. I can see if you were losing. Besides, I got my 18 points and 6 assists. I'm good for now," Jayrode says.

"Yeah man, you are funny, so let me get back to this game and finish it up. Talk to you after the game," says Jayvorn.

"Yeah, you got it, I'll be right here waiting on you," Jayrode replies, laughing and watching his teammates run back onto the court.

Before you know it, the buzzer sounds and the game is over. 77 to 39. It was a blowout! The crowd is going wild and a group of onlookers have run onto the basketball court and lifted Jayvorn and Jayrode up. The two boys pointed at one another and said: "Two to the right!"

The Park

The next morning at the basketball court in the park, Jayvorn is there stretching and warming up as he sees Jayrode coming into the park. "What's up, man? I thought you weren't going to make it," Jayvorn says to Jayrode.

"What? Why would you think that?" Jayrode asks him.

"You are late, and you aren't running," Jayvorn answers him with a smug look on his face.

"I know, I know I will give you your two laps later. Let's just get warmed up," Jayrode answers, putting his bag down next to Jayvorn's and shaking his head. The boys then get started. They warm up and stretch their legs and muscles.

"What's up Jayrode, what happen last night?" Jayvorn asks him.

"What do you mean what happen?" Jayrode asks him.

"I mean why did you leave in the middle of the game last night, Jayrode?"

"Look man, I just had to do something important last night, that's all!" Jayrode answers him in an upsetting voice.

"So what was it, if it was so important?" Jayvorn asks trying to find out what it was. The two have been friends for a long time and tell each other everything. Jayvorn just can't understand why he won't tell him. He looks at his best friend and waits for an answer.

14

"Look, I said it was nothing. Besides I got back to the game before it was over," Jayrode tells him in a more upsetting voice.

"Yeah, you got back to the game, but...."

"Look Jayvorn! Are we going to work out or talk about what I did last night?"

"You're right. That's not my concern. Let's get started," Jayvorn says as he shakes his shoulders. The boys begin to run around the park.

"So Jayvorn, how did you do last night at the game?" Jayrode asks him.

"What! Why are you asking about last night?" Jayvorn asks with a smile on his face.

"You know what I mean, how much did you score last night?" Jayrode asks, trying to be humble.

"Well, after you left and scored your little 14 points...." Jayvorn was saying.

"No, that's 18 points and 6 assists."

"Well, your 18 points and 6 assists; your boy had 27 points and 10 assists! Just a little thing to a giant like me!" Jayvorn says as he was bragging with a big smile on his face as they came back into the park from running around it.

"Oh, don't act like you are all that because if I was in the game, I would have scored 30 points and 15 assists on those bums!" Jayrode says with his chest poked out, as he grabs the basketball out of his bag.

"Oh, that's the key word, if you would have been in the game! But you weren't and we will never know, now will we?" Jayvorn says in a joking way. They begin to do basketball drills, such as

15

layups and chest passes.

Standing on the court doing chest passes, Jayrode looks to Jayvorn and says, "Yo man, I can't believe how the Coach didn't want to put me back in the game for the second half. I could have scored at least fifteen points on them!"

"Well you know how the coach is, and he was really mad at you for leaving in the middle of the game. Besides I thought you didn't want to talk about last night," Jayvorn says in a puzzling way.

"I don't, but I did want to finish the game," Jayrode says.

"I know, I wanted you to finish the game with me, but the Coach didn't let you," Jayvorn says sadly as they are still doing their drills.

"Man, that game was a blowout. I bet it will go down in the record books as the highest scoring game in the league. We scored what, about 40 points on them, and in a championship game," Jayrode says shaking his head.

"Yeah, you're about right, 38 points to be exact," Jayvorn says.

"Man, if I only could have gotten back into the game, we could have scored one hundred points on them," Jayrode says with a touch of anger.

"Yeah, we just wouldn't know. But I do know one thing that will go down in the record books," Jayvorn says smiling.

"Yeah, what's that?" Jayrode asks.

"You, leaving in the middle of a championship game. I know that never happened before, especially to the coach. He'll never forget it!" Jayvorn says laughing.

"Yeah, you're right, but I had to go," Jayrode says.

"So what's up, are you thinking about the MVP awards tomorrow?" Jayvorn asks.

"Oh, man you're right, I forgot all about that, especially after last night. I know I blew it," Jayrode says with his head down upset with himself.

"Yep, I know you did too, and the way you were going you had it in the bag and me beat too," Jayvorn says.

"Don't even talk about it. I know you got it now for sure," Jayrode says real disgusted.

"So I guess you'll be going to the awards ceremony at the church tomorrow," Jayvorn asks.

"Yeah, you know I'll be there, my moms too," Jayrode tells him as he nods his head up and down.

"Yo Jayvorn, what else do we have to do now, because I don't feel so good now," Jayrode says looking sad.

"All we have now is 25 suicides and we can play one-on-one or run two-on-two on the short courts," Jayvorn says as he points to the other side of the park where there are other boys playing basketball.

"Yeah, I think winning a few games of two-on-two will make me feel better. I'll race you in these suicides," Jayrode says. "Go!" Jayrode yells as he takes off to the other side of the basketball court.

Awards

At the church, just before service, Jayvorn, his mother Clara and father Edd are talking to some of their friends and members of their church. Jayvorn sees Jayrode and his mom coming up the block.

"I'll be right back dad," Jayvorn says as he started to run across the street.

"Where are you going?" his dad asks him.

"To see my boy Jayrode right over there."

"Jayvorn, they are coming to church, right boy?" his mom Clara asks him as he ran across the street to meet them. He shook his head yes and waved back to his mom.

One of the church members, Rebecca an older woman is standing next to Jayvorn's parents and some other church members as she says, "Well there goes the neighborhood."

"What do you mean by that?" Edd asks her.

"Oh you don't know about that girl," Rebecca answers him with a look of shock and sarcasm.

"What about that girl?" Clara asks her.

"It is just that she's young and had her son young and she doesn't even know who his father is. You know she was sleeping with so many guys at that time," one of the other church members said as he shook his head and his wife grabbed his arm.

"Oh man, please. So, she made a few mistakes in her life. It looks like she's doing a fine job raising her son by herself," Jayvorn's dad tells him.

"Well, all I hear is she's out to get a man or a

18

dad for that boy. And mine's not up for grabs," Rebecca says as she grabs her husband's arm tighter and pulls him, while the other couple looks over at Jayvorn, Jayrode, and his mother and shake their heads.

"Rebecca, please! Don't no one want your sad excuse for a husband," Clara twists her lips up with a frown and as she starts to walk off.

Susan, the other woman there with her nose in the air, says, "I don't know about all that. All I know is she has no job, no money, and living in the projects and gets welfare," as she grabs her husband.

"Susan, please. Like you never been on welfare. We all have at one time or another," Clara tells her with an attitude.

"I can't believe you all. The woman is just doing what she can to raise her son in the right way. Besides her son is a good kid, and he helped all your boys get to and win the championship game," Edd says to them as his wife walks away to meet Jayrode and his mom.

"You all know what is so funny? I bet you all don't even know her name! But you all know everything bad about her, "Edd says in disgust as he walks away.

"Hey Cindy," Edd says trying to get his wife's attention. "Hold on baby!" He yells to her as she looks back at him. He catches up to her and the two of them walk over to meet Jayvorn, Jayrode and his mother.

"I can't believe them!" Clara says to Edd in

19

an angry voice.

"Don't let that get to you," Edd tells her looking at the angry expression on his wife's face.

"Hey Cindy," Clara says as they walk up to them.

"Hey Clara, hey Edd," Cindy said to them as she greets them with a hug and kiss. While Jayvorn and Jayrode run across the street back to the church.

"What are you doing over here girl? Are you going to church or not?" Clara asks Cindy, smiling at her.

"Yeah I am, but you know," Cindy answers in a shy and humble voice.

"Oh girl, please, people are going to always talk," Clara says with her lips twisted up and with a frown on her face as she looks at Susan and Rebecca with their husbands.

"Besides, they talked about Jesus," Clara said as they both looked across the street at them going into the church.

"You're right girl, and I know, but it's not me, I can handle it. It's my son, you know. He's a kid, my baby. He doesn't need to hear or go through all that," Cindy said to them.

"Come on, Cindy I know you don't want to miss today. Our boys are getting championship trophies today. Besides, he is not a baby, he is a young man. Look at him he knows what is going on in his life," Edd says to Cindy as they go across the street while everyone enters the church.

As they enter the church, they find their sons sitting with the rest of the team in the front row.

The choir has just finished singing hymns. The pastor gets up to the pulpit as everyone takes their seats.

"Can I get an Amen, for the choir?" the pastor asks.

"Amen," everyone said.

"Can I get an Amen?"

"Amen!"

"Well, I'm not going to preach a long sermon today."

"Amen!" someone in the church shouts. The whole church starts to laugh.

"Yeah I know I can get an Amen, for that too," the pastor says, as he starts to laugh and shakes his head. "But we have a long day today. Because these fine boys won the All-State Championship and we've got some awards to give out. Come on, stand up so the whole church can see you." The church clap and grin with pride as the entire team stands up.

"Settle down, settle down," the pastor tells the church as they take their seats. "We will have the reading of the Word by Sister Young, who will also do the announcements. Following that, the choir will give us a few lovely hymn selections. Immediately after the tithe and offering, I will give you all the Word from the Lord and then I will hand it over to Deacon Brown who is the basketball coach that led these fine boys to the championship and won it Friday night. He will be giving out the award trophies. Immediately after all that, we will be going downstairs for an awards dinner for these

21

fine boys. I know the ladies of the church worked hard on that dinner, so we are not going to hold them up too long, or let the food get cold. By that time I know everyone will be hungry. And I don't know about you all, but I don't want any cold fried chicken!" the Pastor says and everyone in the church laughs.

"So without further delay, can I get an Amen, for Sister Young?" the Pastor asks.

"Amen," the church said, as Sister Young walks to the pulpit.

"Amen, church," says Sister Young as she prepares to read from her Bible. After reading the announcements, the service continues. The choir sings three songs. Then did praise and worship not only praising God for what He is doing in their own personal lives but in the lives of the young men.

The congregation is now walking around placing their tithes and offering in the baskets that sit on a table at the front of the church. As each of them pass the group of boys sitting on the front row some walk by and smile.

The pastor stands and begins to preach and the boys become restless. Although the pastor said he would be short it seems like forever to the boys as the anticipation of receiving their awards grows. Jayrode taps Jayvorn as pastor begins to introduce Coach Brown as to say, "It's time!"

As they wait for Coach Brown to stand up and start calling their names, so they could get their trophies. Jayvorn and Jayrode are really waiting to see who was going to get the MVP award. Before the boys even know it, the pastor was looking down at them and he says:

"I know these boys have been waiting a long time and have been as patient as they could be, so can I get an Amen, for Deacon Brown?"

"Amen," the church says as the pastor sits down and Coach Brown stands up in front of the church. Two ladies come from the back room with a cart with nine small trophies, one large trophy, and two plaques. The ladies roll the cart to the front of the church right beside the coach.

"Now these boys went through a lot to get here and worked very hard, so when I call your name, come on up and get your trophy, so everyone can see you. First off is Michael," says Coach Brown and the church starts to clap as he gets up.

"Next, we have David, Paul, and Donte, oh Lord; here go these funny named kids. Now parents, can I ask why do you name your kids names we can't say and they can't spell?" Coach Brown asks and everyone starts to laugh.

"I'm just joking, don't get mad at me. I didn't name these kids. Now we have Tequin, Dayday, and Stefen…" says Coach.

"No, that's Steffon," the boy says as he gets up to the coach and corrects him.

The coach says, "I'm sorry, you see, that's Steffon," as he gives him his trophy.

"Now these last two boys worked the hardest, and I have to say they have the funniest names. They should have been brothers for their names are so close. We are always getting them mixed up: Jayvorn and Jayrode. Now, these two boys made it real hard for me to give them this next award, so we decided to give two awards. So, MVP 1 goes to Jayvorn and MVP 2 goes to Jayrode," the Coach says as he hands the boys the two plaques. Everyone in the church is now standing and cheering for the boys.

"Now this big championship trophy will stay here in the church for display," Coach Brown says. Everyone in their excitement begins to walk to the front of the church where the boys are with their trophy and where the large trophy has been placed.

"Settle down now, settle down. Remember we have to go downstairs to eat. The ladies of the church fixed everyone a lovely dinner for the boys winning," the pastor says. Everyone begins to move toward the door, so they can go downstairs and continue the celebration and eat.

As they walk downstairs, Jayvorn laughing says to Jayrode, "Yo Jayrode, you know you should have gotten the MVP 1 award cause you're better than me. Only by a little!"

"Yeah, you're right. But that's ok at least I got an MVP award. Besides after what I did in the last game, you earned it," Jayrode says to him as he gives Jayvorn five as everyone goes downstairs to eat.

The Good News

Two days later, Clara is home by herself, fixing dinner for Edd and Jayvorn. The phone rings. "Hold on! Hold on! I'm coming, I'm coming!" she says to herself as the phone rings again and again. "Now why is it whenever you are in the middle of doing something, someone wants to call or come by Lord," Clara finishes saying to herself as she gets to the phone. "Hello?"

"Hello, is this the Hall's residence?" a man on the other end asks.

"Yes, can I help you?" Clara asks with a confusing look on her face.

"Yes, I got your name and number from Coach Brown. I would like to say I love and saw your son play basketball...." the man says.

"Excuse me, may I ask who you are?"

"I'm sorry my name is Coach Davis from Clark's Men Academy. Like I said before, I saw your son play last week and I enjoyed the way he handled himself and the way he played with his teammates."

"Well, thank you, I appreciate that. He does work hard and he is a good boy."

"Yes, I see that. That's why I have talked to my colleagues and we all agreed that your son, Jayvorn, is that his name?"

"Yes, it is."

"Well, Jayvorn would be perfect for our scholarship program."

Clara gets excited, "Excuse me, is this like a

college or something?"

"No, Mrs. Hall. We are not a college. We are a high school, a private school. But 99% of our students graduate and go to college with honors," Mr. Davis lets her know.

"Ok, I'm listening. You've got my attention. So, what does this have to do with my son and playing basketball?", Clara replies as she feels there is more to this.

"Well, Mrs. Hall, it's like this. We would like for your son to come play for us. In return, we will give him a fine education with a chance to go to some of the top universities or colleges that have basketball programs."

"That's fine, really good. Now, what's the catch?" Clara asks as she is all excited with a voice as if something is fishy.

"I'm glad you asked Mrs. Hall. All Jayvorn has to do is maintain a C+ average and score an 85 on a placement test. That's all and he's in!"

"That's not too hard if that is all he has to do."

"Yes, that's all."

"Ok, now I'll have to talk this over with my husband and see how he feels about it," Clara tells him all happy.

"That would be great. I would love to meet and talk to both of you and Jayvorn. As well as bring over some brochures of our school, basketball program- along with our academic program."

"Well, my husband is off tomorrow and Jayvorn gets home from school by 5pm, so would you like to come by tomorrow?"

"That will be fine. I can come by tomorrow by 4pm. That will give us some time to talk before Jayvorn comes and I meet him."

"Yes, that does sound good. Here's my address: it's 102 Tinton Street and I'll see you tomorrow."

"Here's my information if you have any problems, you and your husband can call me. It's 555-2857. Thank you, Mrs. Hall."

"No, thank you, Mr. Davis!" They hung up the phone. Clara jumps up and down as she let out a loud "Yes! Yes! Yes! Thank you, Jesus!" She says as looks around as if she couldn't wait for her husband to come home.

Later that day Jayvorn is home doing homework. Clara is walking back and forth checking on him.

"Do you need help with anything," she asks him excited and giddy as a schoolgirl, looking at him smiling.

"No mom. Are you ok?" He asks her in a nice voice with a puzzled look on his face as if he knows she is up to something but doesn't know what.

"Ok baby, you let me know if you need me to help you with anything. You know I am good at school work," she says with excitement as she is looking at him.

The front door opens. Edd comes in from work, as he drops his bag at the door. Clara runs to him. "Edd!" She grabs his arm, taking him into their room. She closes the door behind them and starts kissing him all over his face and lips.

"Hold on, hold on baby. I just got home," Edd says as he kisses her back. "What's got into you, Clara?"

"Edd, I just love you and my son. He made me so happy to be his mother today," she tells him with a big smile on her face.

"What are you talking about?" He says as he tries to hold her back.

"Oh, Edd, I just love you, I love you, I love you!" She tells him as she keeps kissing him.

"Ok baby, hold on, hold on, I just got in the door," Edd starts taking off his shirt and unbuttoning his pants as he backs up from her.

"Edd, I'm not talking about all that," she says as she rebuttons his pants and put his shirt back on.

"What! So, what are you talking about?" he asks her looking puzzled.

"I got a call today!" She tells him all excited.

"And," he says, funnily looking at her, raising his eyebrows.

"I got a call today from a man!"

"A man! What man?" he asks in a hard and serious voice.

"A coach, Edd," she says twisting her lips up.

"Ok, a coach, what coach?" he asks.

"Look Edd, are you going to let me tell you?" she asks him.

"Well woman, tell me!" he says, looking

puzzled, trying to find out what is going on.

"If you are going to act like that, I'm not going to tell you!" She says folding her arms, looking at him seriously.

"Ok, Ok, I'm going to sit here on the bed and let you talk," he tells her and sits down.

"Well, like I was saying, I got a call today from this man who is a coach. He tells me he wants Jayvorn to go to this private school and everything."

"What!" Edd said. "We can't afford a private school. What is wrong with the school he is in now?" Edd asks her.

"Edd, did you understand what I just told you?"

"No, all you're telling me is bits and pieces. Maybe if you calm down and tell me everything, I will know what you are talking about," he tells her.

"Ok, there you go again, do you want to hear what I've got to say or not?" She tells him looking down at him on the bed.

"Ok Clara, Ok, go ahead," he replies as he rolls his eyes and shakes his head. "Ok, back to the beginning. As you know, he called me today. He said he liked the way Jayvorn plays basketball. He was at his last game last week, and he talked to the people at the school and they all agreed Jayvorn would be good for their scholarship program. He would go to a private school and graduate with a chance to go to college or a university with a basketball program. All he has to do is keep a B average and score an 85 on a placement test, and he's in. We don't have to pay nothing. He just has to play basketball for them."

"So, what if he doesn't play the way they want or good enough for them. Do they drop him and send him back to his old school?" he asks her.

"I don't know all that. That's why the coach is coming here to meet you and me tomorrow at 4:00 pm so you can ask him everything."

"So, what does Jayvorn have to say about all this?" he asks her as he took her by the hands.

"I didn't tell him yet. I wanted to wait until we find out everything. Then we let him know. I do know this, if he does go and graduate from that school, he'll get into a better college than the community college." Clara tells him as she sits on his lap and gives him a kiss.

"Well, you got a point there," Edd holds her and kisses her back.

"Come on now Edd!" she says as she jumps up and starts to the door.

"What! Come on baby, I am in the mood now!" He tells her as he grabs her hand and tries to pull her back to the bed.

"Not now Edd, you know he's up in his room!" She says with a smile on her face getting up from his lap.

"Yeah, and we're in ours, with the door closed!" He tells her with a strained look on his face.

"Come on Edd, besides I got dinner ready. Just put it up until tonight!" She tells him as she gives him a kiss on the cheek and pats his chest. She opens the room door and goes to the kitchen.

"I can't believe this woman! Got me all excited and ready to go, then tells me to wait till later!" Edd says to himself, as he shook his head and buttoned his shirt back.

"Dinner is ready boys!" Clara yells with a grin and a hint of laughter in her voice, as she knows her husband is all hot and bothered; all worked up over her because she still got it going on.

The Meeting

The next morning Edd is in the bathroom washing up. Jayvorn is in the kitchen fixing him something to eat.

"Good morning big daddy," Clara says with a smile on her face.

"Good morning little momma!" Edd tells her with a bigger smile and a grin on his face as he gives her a kiss and pats her on the butt.

"Alright now, don't start none! Won't be none!" She tells him, smiling at him.

"Mom, dad, I will see you all later. I'm going to school now," Jayvorn yells to his parents, as he grabs his black bag and heads to the front door.

"Hey Jayvorn, I need you to come straight home after school," Edd yells to him from the bathroom.

"But dad, I got practice after school," he answers his dad, while he is at the door.

"I know, but right after that I need you to come home. Your mom and I have a surprise for you," he tells Jayvorn, as Clara smiles at Edd.

"What is it?" he asked with a smile on his face.

"It's just someone we want you to meet."

"Ok dad, I see you after practice," Jayvorn says as he goes out the door with no care of what is in store for him.

In the park after school, Jayvorn and Jayrode

are warming up to start their workout, stretching their legs and muscles.

"Yo, Jayvorn! What's up with you man?" Jayrode asks him because he looks like something was bothering him.

"Nothing, why?" he asks Jayrode.

"It looks like you got a lot on your mind and you look like you are not here," Jayrode tells him as they start to run around the park.

"It's nothing, I just have to get home early today," Jayvorn tells him as he shakes his head and looks really puzzled.

"Why, what's up?" he asks him.

"That's the thing. I don't know," Jayvorn answers him all puzzled.

"What do you mean, you don't know?" he asks again.

"Like I said, I don't know. My dad just told me he needs me to come home early today," Jayvorn says as the boys were running around the park.

"So, what do you think it is?" Jayrode asks.

"That's it, I don't know. It's not my birthday or holiday I know of," he says to him.

"So, maybe it's got something to do with your mom and dad?" Jayrode asks trying to find out what it was.

"No, it's not that because I checked my calendar. Nothing was on it for today," Jayvorn tells him.

"I'm not talking about that!" Jayrode says to him.

"So, what!" Jayvorn asks with a funny look on his face as they came running into the park.

"Maybe your mom is having a baby!" Jayrode tells him.

"What! My mom, pregnant, please!" he says with a shocking look on his face as he grabs the basketball out of his bag. They begin to do their basketball drills.

"Why not, what's wrong with your dad?" Jayrode asks him as he starts to laugh.

"Nothing! But my mom, she would have told me about that last night. Besides, my dad said he wants me to meet someone. I don't think they could have had a baby that fast!" he answers Jayrode as they started to do layups.

Edd and Clara are getting ready to meet Coach Davis. Edd is in the room trying to fix his tie. Clara is in the bathroom fixing her makeup.

"Hey baby, is everything fixed nice for the man?" Clara asks Edd from the bathroom.

"Yes dear, I took everything you gave me and set it out in the living room," Edd answers from the bedroom.

"Are you sure we have chips, juice, tea, cake, and fruit out for the man?" she asks Edd again.

"Look Clara, I put everything you gave me out. It's enough food and drinks to have a dinner party," Edd told her. He was getting frustrated with his tie.

"Oh my Lord, coffee! You know how those coaches love to drink coffee," she says in a shocking voice.

"I got a pot already made. The one I was just drinking from. Now please Clara, stop worrying about all that and come here and help me with my tie," Edd tells her in a furious voice.

"Oh Edd, come here," she said as she walks in the bedroom with Edd.

"What would you ever do without me?", she said as she walks over to Edd and he turns to her so she could fix his tie.

"The same thing you would do without me," he answers her as she was fixing his tie.

"What's that?" she said. "Go ahead and say something smart. Just remember I got your necktie in my hands!" She tells him with her lips twisted up looking at him seriously with her eyebrows lifted, with one hand on the bow and the other on the legs of his tie, ready to pull if he said something smart.

"Be miserable!" He said as he kisses her on the lips and laughs.

"Oh please, boy, I'm not going to be miserable. You might be, but not me. Happy yes, miserable, I don't think so!" She says to him in a smart voice. As she twists her lips up and rolls her eyes and head, she throws his tie legs into his chest and walks off to the other side of the room. At that time, the doorbell rings. Edd goes out of the room and starts down the hall to the front door.

"It's your coach," Edd yells back to Clara as he walks down the hallway to the door.

"Well, get it!" she says still in her sarcastic voice.

"No, wait, wait, wait Edd. Do I look ok?" she asks him in a nervously and shaking voice, as she runs into the hallway behind Edd.

"Well Edd! Look at me. Do I look ok?" she asks again so Edd can see her.

Edd turns his head quickly at her. "Yes dear, you look fine," he says as he gets to the door.

"But Edd wait, you didn't even see me!" She says with her hands up at her side like she is surprised.

Edd looks at her again and twists his lips up and shakes his head at her, then opens the door.

"How are you?" Edd says to the man at the door.

"Fine. How are you?" Mr. Davis says. Then says, "Mr. Hall, I believe?"

As Mr. Davis comes into their house, Edd closes the door. Mr. Davis introduces himself to Clara and they go into the living room.

While back at the park: "Look man, maybe they are going to adopt a kid," Jayrode tells Jayvorn as they start to do other basketball drills. "And the guy you are going to meet is bringing him over."

"Adopt! Please, look man, it don't have nothing to do with no kid or baby!", Jayvorn tells him in a serious voice.

"So what do you think it is?" he asks him.

"That's the thing. I don't know!" Jayvorn answers.

"Well, look it's not your birthday, no holiday, not a baby or kid, and it's not your mom or dad's birthday or nothing to do with them, so maybe you're in trouble," Jayrode tells him with a serious look and a smile on his face.

"That's what I thought. But I don't remember doing nothing wrong!" Jayvorn says.

"So maybe it's something you didn't do," Jayrode says.

"Like what. I checked over everything I was supposed to do last week," Jayvorn answers him.

"Well maybe your mom found something in your room or in your books or your bag from school," Jayrode said.

"Like what?" Jayvorn asks.

"Like some weed or dirty pictures or something," Jayrode says with his hand to his mouth like he was smoking something.

"What! You know better than that. What's the number one rule?" Jayvorn says with a real serious voice.

"No drugs!" they both say at the same time.

"I know, I know, I'm just playing with you," Jayrode says as they are finishing up their basketball drills.

"Look here, everyone was so worried about me, and what I had to do the other night, now you are the one with the big secret," Jayrode tells him as he puts the ball up.

"Man please! I don't even know what it is," Jayvorn tells him.

"Don't sweat it, you will be alright. Now what else do we have to do?" Jayrode asks him.

"All we have to do is our suicides," Jayvorn answers as he pats Jayrode on the chest as to say,

"Let's get this done."

"Go!" Jayvorn says as he runs up the basketball court, with Jayrode standing there looking.

"Oh, you are funny now!", Jayrode says as he starts to run behind him.

Back at Edd and Clara's house, Mr. Davis is sitting in the living room with Edd and Clara, with all his brochures and paper laid out.

"As you can see Mr. Hall, we have at Clark's Men Academy some of the finest academic and sports programs out. We have the best science, math and, reading programs, as well as music and arts programs. So you can see your son will get a full education as well as he will fully develop his basketball skills," Mr. Davis explains to Edd and Clara, who are sitting across the table from him.

"That's all good and it sounds like a real fine school. Let me ask you this, what if my son can't play as good as you need or expect him to do?" Edd asks him, as he looks at the brochure Mr. Davis passed him.

"Excuse me, Mr. Hall. What do you mean by that?" Mr. Davis asks him.

"I mean, what if the kids in your school don't like my son or the way he plays, what then, do you just drop him from your program?" Edd asks him as he looks at the kids in the brochure.

"Oh no, Mr. Hall. It is not what you think. We at Clark's Men Academy are an integrated school. Our basketball team is 50% black and 50% white. Just like most of our campuses, we have kids

38

from all over the country," Mr. Davis tells him.

"That's good at least he won't be the only one there by himself," Clara says.

"No, it's not like that. He won't be the first and only minority in the school. Our scholarship program is for all our programs, not just for basketball. As long as a kid has the will and drive to want to learn we will see that he or she learns. We love helping them succeed in life," he tells Clara.

"Well, that's good to know, because I would hate to take him out of his school where he can get all he needs to put him in your school only for you to drop him or he drops out because he doesn't play good enough for you," Edd says.

"I understand how you feel, Mr. Hall. I assure you that as long as Jayvorn wants to succeed in life we will be here. Our staff doesn't mind staying late to help a kid. We also have great tutors, and study groups for kids who love to work with one another," Mr. Davis says with a smile on his face as if to say he was proud of his school.

"Like I explained to your wife on the phone earlier, we at Clark's Men have a 99% rate of our kids going to some of the best colleges and universities and every year we hold a 100 % graduation rate. That means everyone at Clark's Men graduates," he tells them very proudly.

"That sounds real good, so tell us more about this scholarship program. How does it work? Will my son have to stay on campus or what?" Clara asks all excited as she looks at a different brochures Edd just passed her.

"Well Mr. and Mrs. Hall, it's like this, as long as Jayvorn keeps C + average and scores a 78 or higher on his placement test, we will provide everything he needs. We will pay in full his tuition, all his books, and his alma-mater jacket," Mr. Davis informs them.

"Alma-mater! What's that?" Edd asks looking puzzled.

"It's the school patch, as you can see everyone is wearing it on their jackets," he tells Edd.

"Ok, that is good, but still, does my son have to stay on campus?" Clara asks again as she is looking through the brochures in her hand that have kids living on campus and in dorm rooms.

"Yes, we do have dorms on campus, but in Jayvorn's case, no he won't have to stay on campus," he answers.

Edd looks up at Mr. Davis as to say what's wrong with my son staying on campus.

"It's only an hour and a half by train or two and a half to three hours by bus. I know this because we have a young lady who lives not too far from here, who goes to our school," he tells Clara with a smile.

"That's good. I wonder who she is." Clara asks Coach Davis.

The front door opens. "Mom, dad, I'm home!" Jayvorn yells as he comes in the door and puts his bag down.

"We are in the living room baby. Come in here," Clara calls back to him.

"What is it you need me for?" he calls out as he goes down the hallway to the living room. As he looks down the hallway into the living room, he sees a white man sitting in the living room. He looks at him with a puzzled look on his face as he enters the living room. He sees his mom and dad sitting on the other side of the table, Mr. Davis stands up and stretches out his hand to greet him.

"Jayvorn, I presume," Mr. Davis says to Jayvorn as he shakes his hand. "How are you young man?", Mr. Davis asks him as they are still shaking hands.

Jayvorn looks at his mom and dad with a still puzzled look as they are sitting down at the table with all the brochures and papers out in front of them. He stands there looking at his mom and dad and back at Mr. Davis. He turns to Mr. Davis and says, "I'm fine and you are?"

"Jayvorn, this is Mr. Davis. He is a coach," Clara answers him.

"A coach!" Jayvorn says as he looks back at his mom with a surprised look on his face.

"Yes, my name is Coach Davis of Clark's Men Academy. I was just telling your mom and dad all about our school and how we would love to have you with us," Mr. Davis says to Jayvorn.

As Jayvorn walks over and stands behind his mom, he looks down at all the brochures on the table.

"Clark's Men Academy. What's that some kind of college?" Jayvorn asks as he picks up one of the brochures.

"No, it's not a college," Mr. Davis says with laughter in his voice. "Son, it's a fine high school, one of the best! It has a lot to offer you."

High school! I'm already in high school," Jayvorn says with a questionable voice and a puzzled look on his face.

"I know son, but this is a private school that has everything you need to help you get into college. Most of all, it has a really good basketball team," Clara says to Jayvorn as she looks up at him.

"What, with a bunch of preppy kids!" Jayvorn says with his eyes wide open. "Come on dad. I'm in the beginning of my senior year and I'm already on my basketball team, who is going to take this year's finals and all my friends, dad!" Jayvorn says as he looks at his dad who stands up and looks at him.

"I know Jayvorn, that's why your mother and I are going to leave this up to you, but we do want you to hear Mr. Davis out, then you can decide," Edd explains to him.

"Ok dad, but I mean…," Jayvorn says as he looks at Mr. Davis and shook his head and sat in his father's seat, next to his mom.

Mr. Davis starts to tell him everything he has told his mom and dad about the school.

"So if I do go to this school, how would that affect my grades?" Jayvorn asks him.

"Well, since you are in your senior year, you would take a placement test and all your credits will follow you from your old school to this one. You will still graduate this year with our senior class,"

Mr. Davis lets him know.

"Ok, so how is your team?" Jayvorn asks. "I mean; I don't know anything about these guys. It took us at least two years to get our team together. That's why we work so well and flow. I'm saying what if they don't take to me coming in as a senior, playing for one year and leave?" he asks, as his dad looks down at him shocked to see his son asking an intelligent question.

"That's a good question, Jayvorn. Like I was telling your mom and dad, we have a great group of guys who get along with everyone and everything. Most importantly our varsity team is mostly seniors who will be leaving next year right along with you," Mr. Davis answers him.

"So you are saying, I go to your school, play on your team and graduate with your senior class. That is all good, but how does that help me get to the NBA?" Jayvorn asks him, as his mom, dad, and Mr. Davis starts to laugh.

"I mean, my coach has been telling me that this year he is going to introduce me to some college scout, who can help me go pro," Jayvorn says as they were laughing at the way he said it.

"Look son, I'm glad that you are looking out for your future. That's a good thing. In our division, college scouts are at all our games. By the time we get to the championship games you will have all the scouts trying to introduce themselves to you, trying to find out who you are," Mr. Davis tells him.

As Edd smiles and starts to like the school more and Clara is so excited you can see it all over her face, she tries to hold back her smile.

"So what are you saying, Mr. Davis? You'll help my son get into a good college or university, even though we might not be able to afford it?" Edd asks him.

"Mr. Hall, this is how this works; when the time comes and it will come soon. We will have our excellent counselors help Jayvorn with everything he needs to go to the best college or university he wants, with the best scholarship that is out there for him," Mr. Davis says as he looks up at Edd in his eyes, with a straight face, then everyone looks at Jayvorn.

"Well dad, like you always say, whatever don't hurt me, makes me stronger!" Jayvorn says as he nodded his head and stretched out his hand to Mr. Davis.

"You got a deal," he tells him.

"Well son, congratulations! I think you're making one of the best choices of your life," Mr. Davis says as he shakes Jayvorn's hand. "Now all we have to do is get you down to the school so you can take your placement test and get your grades from your other school."

"So when will he start at your school?" Clara asks.

"If you can get Jayvorn to the school this week, he takes the test, by Monday we will have his scores and his grades from his school. He can start then," Mr. Davis answers her with a smile.

"What? Monday, why so soon?" Jayvorn asks as he looks at Mr. Davis pulling some papers out of his briefcase.

"Well, we would like for you to get to know the school and all your classes before our first basketball tournament," Mr. Davis tells him as he hands the papers to Clara, so she can read and sign them.

"So when is your first tournament?" Jayvorn asks him.

"In a few weeks or so, just right around the end of the month," Mr. Davis tells him.

"Man, that's early. By that time we'll just be starting tryouts," Jayvorn tells him.

"I know, here's the thing. We are a division A team and your old school is a division C team, so we play two different leagues. So you don't have to worry about playing your old teammates and betraying them because we will never play in the same leagues. That's why we start our game sooner than they do, and we play more games than them. We have four tournaments, then the playoffs and finally the championship games. You see Jayvorn, that's why your old school will play everyone, one time and then go to the finals. We play everyone one or two times, then go to the playoffs, and then the championship games," Mr. Davis explains to Jayvorn.

"Ok, now I see! Because I was kind of feeling bad about playing against my friends and all," Jayvorn says while his mom and dad were finishing up reading the papers Mr. Davis gave them.

Edd asks, "Where do we need to sign?" as

Mr. Davis points out all the spaces.

The Practice

Saturday, two days later, Jayrode is in the park warming up as he is waiting on Jayvorn. He is late getting to the park. As Jayrode looks up, he sees Jayvorn coming down the block.

"I thought you weren't coming," Jayrode tells Jayvorn, as Jayvorn was coming into the park.

"What do you mean, it's Saturday, right?" Jayvorn replies.

"Yeah, but I don't see you running," Jayrode said joking with him as they gave each other five.

"Yeah, I know, I know, I owe you two laps," Jayvorn said with a bad look on his face as if something was wrong with him. And it was because now he had to tell his best friend that he is going to a new school.

"Yo man, I'm just messing with you. Besides you can call us even because I still owe you two laps from the other day," he tells him laughing.

"That's ok!" Jayvorn says as he sat on the benches with a sad look on his face.

"Yo man, what's up?" Jayrode asks him as he saw he had a lot on his mind.

"Nothing," Jayvorn answers him, trying to find a nice way to tell him he is going to a new school.

"So, what happened the other day? I didn't see you in school the last two days?" Jayrode asks as he sat next to him.

"You're not going to believe this," Jayvorn

said shaking his head.

"Believe what?" Jayrode asks, looking at him to find out what was happening.

"The other day I got home and there's a coach in my living room with my mom and dad…" he starts to say.

"A college coach?" Jayrode asked as he interrupted him.

"No, that's what I thought, but he was a high school coach from Clark's Men Academy. He told my mom and dad all about this school, and they want me to go, not only go but play on their basketball team. Here's the funny part, they are going to pay for everything."

"What? Is this some kind of private school with a bunch of preppy kids?" Jayrode asks with a surprised look on his face.

"Something like that, but it is all kind of kids from all over," he tells Jayrode.

"So how did they hear about you?" Jayrode asks.

"I don't know. The way my mom told me, he was at the championship game and saw me play. He liked what he saw," Jayvorn tells him.

"See man, I know I should have stayed and played that whole game. Damn, that's why coach didn't want me to play in the second half. He knew that the coach would have seen my skills and sign me on the spot," Jayrode said in a mad voice, as he thought about the coach not letting him play.

"Look, Jayrode, I don't know how long he was at the game. He might have seen you play in

48

the first half. You did dominate the beginning of the game," Jayvorn tells him.

"Yeah, you are right about that, but still, I don't know why coach hated on me and didn't put me in," Jayrode says still angry.

"Remember, you left the game at halftime," Jayvorn says to him.

"Yeah, you're right, but still," Jayrode replies.

"Well, look, if Coach had something to do with it he would have told him about you because everyone knows how good you are. Besides they might be trying to get in touch with you now!" Jayvorn tells him.

"Yeah, maybe I should go home and see," Jayrode says excitedly, as he bounces the basketball hard to the ground.

"Man, I'm just playing, but that's good news. Yo so tell me all about this preppy school," he asks Jayvorn.

"Yo, it's tight. It's like a college, but a high school. It has five buildings, a big track and field, and a football and soccer field. They were playing some weird game out there. Yo, listen, the school is one big building, then the lunchroom is another building, and the library is another building there's another building for music, arts, and drama. They do plays and stuff. Then in the back, there's a big building that is the gym. Man, you should have seen this gym. It looks like a coliseum. It has real bleachers on both sides of the floor and a real scoreboard like in the NBA," he describes.

49

"What, no wooden bleachers and flashcard scoreboard?" Jayrode says joking with him.

"No, for real. Finish telling me about this coliseum gym and don't forget about the honeys. I know it has some bad looking white chicks up there," Jayrode says.

"Oh, that's the thing. It's got some bad looking sisters as well. Matter of fact one girl lives somewhere in this neighborhood," Jayvorn tells him.

"So do you know who she is?" Jayrode asks him.

"No, but we'll be catching the train at the same time so I will see her soon," Jayvorn answers.

"Yo, when you do, you need to hook a brother up or something," Jayrode asks him, as he stands up.

"Yeah, I will put in a good word for you," Jayvorn answers him as he watches Jayrode bounce the ball between his legs.

"Man, I can't wait until they call me so I can put down my moves in that gym. I bet by the time the year ends they will retire my jersey," Jayrode said with a big smile on his face.

"Boy, you really got jokes," Jayvorn says as he strips him of the basketball.

"Yo, what are we going to do now, practice or what?" Jayrode asks.

"No, I don't feel it today," Jayvorn answers him shaking his head.

"So, what's up," he asks again.

"How about some two on two?" Jayvorn

50

asks as he looks over to the short courts and sees some guys playing.

"Yeah, that's real," Jayrode says as he shakes his head and they start to walk over to the courts. Jayvorn finishes telling Jayrode all about the school and everything.

First Days

Monday morning Jayvorn is at the train station, on his way to his new school for the first time. He yawns as he is still tired and sleepy.

Later that morning, Jayrode is in front of his school with all of his friends, just showing off and having fun.

Later that afternoon at Clark Men's, Jayvorn is stopping to ask some kids how to find some of his classes. As they point to show him, he drops some of his books.

About the same time that afternoon Jayrode is at his locker in the hallway of his school with three of his friends talking and watching everyone go to and from their classes. As Jayrode looks up, he sees Tiffany coming down the hallway. She is smiling and looking at him as she waves and walks by with a sexy model walk, looking real good in a tight shirt and pants, as she goes down the other end of the hallway to her class.

The next morning, Jayvorn is at the train station. He sees a girl wearing the school alma mater. He goes up to her and introduces himself to her and they get to talking as they go to school.

Later that same morning Jayrode is outside his school, as everyone is going in. Tiffany walks up to him and starts flirting with him.

That afternoon, Jayvorn is in the gym locker room meeting his teammates for the first time, as they get changed for practice.

That same afternoon, Jayrode is in the gym at his school playing basketball with his friends, showing off, as he sees Tiffany on the bleachers with her friends watching him, laughing and pointing at him as they are talking to one another.

Trying to Keep the Routine

Wednesday afternoon after school Jayrode is in the park stretching his legs warming up, waiting for Jayvorn to come. As he looks up, he sees Jayvorn running down the block to the park. Jayvorn runs into the park with his alma-mater jacket on. Jayrode looks at him with anger as if he was mad at him or something.

"Sorry I'm late," Jayvorn says to Jayrode as he goes to give him five.

"Yo man, I been here over thirty minutes waiting for you," Jayrode tells him with an angry voice.

"I said I was sorry, and besides you saw me running to get to the park," Jayvorn replies.

"Yeah, you were running," he said as he started to laugh.

"Oh, you got jokes!" Jayvorn says as he took his sweatpants out of his bag.

"You know you looked like a scared fool running in that getup," Jayrode tells him still laughing.

"I don't see anything funny," Jayvorn says as he changes his clothes.

"Yeah, you right. That's why you don't owe me two laps, because whoever seen you running may have thought you were running for your life," Jayrode says joking on him.

"Oh, you really got jokes now!" Jayvorn says as he started to warm up.

"No, but for real, is this how it's going to be, first you start coming late for practice, then you miss one or two. Finally, you just stop coming altogether?" Jayrode asked as they start to run around the park.

"Come on man, you know what we vowed, every Saturday and every Wednesday, no matter what! You got my back and I got yours. Even through college and the NBA, unless we go to different states, and we still will be there for each other," Jayvorn tells him as they are coming into the park to start their drills.

"You right, but with you out there with all those preppy kids, I thought you just might forget about us poor folks," Jayrode tells him.

"Poor folks are those them new Nikes on your feet," Jayvorn says as he looked down at Jayrode's feet with his eyebrows lifted up.

'Ain't nothing poor about them, where did you cop them from," Jayvorn asks him.

"What, these, you like them?" Jayrode asked as he shows them off.

"Yeah, they are tight. How much they put your mom back?" he asked him.

"A little something, something, why, you want me to get you a pair? You know I got the hookup," Jayrode tells him bragging.

"Oh, you got the hookup now. Now that's real funny," Jayvorn says.

"I'm saying, my mom got a new job in the mall and she gets discounts on everything she buys," Jayrode tells him.

"Yeah, that's cool," he said, as they finished up some of their drills.

"What's up baby boy, you looking a little slow there," Jayrode asks him as Jayvorn is kneeling down shaking his head.

"Man, slow is not the word. I'm worn out after all that running I did today," Jayvorn says as he leans on the basketball court pole.

"Look man, all we got to do is chest passes and suicides. After that, run three games of two on two, and that's it for the day," Jayrode tells him.

"Look, after these chest passes and suicides, I'm done for the day," Jayvorn told him as they start their chest passes.

"No pain, no gain, you know how that goes, no pain, no gain," Jayrode says teasing him.

"Look, Jayrode, after today, how about we change our time on Wednesday. We can start an hour later," Jayvorn asks him.

"Yeah, that would be good. So I don't have to wait on you no more," Jayrode tells him as they finish up.

"So what's up, want to race these suicides?" Jayrode asks him.

"No, I'm just going to run them out," Jayvorn answers him as they run up and down the court.

Love Interests

On Thursday morning, Jayvorn meets Tracy at the train station, as they have been doing for the last two days. They are laughing and joking around as they wait for the train to go to school.

Later that morning: Jayrode is running to catch up with Tiffany as she is going into the school. He calls to her. She looks back and stops as all the other kids go in before her. He runs up to her and they both go into the school talking and laughing.

Later that same day: Jayvorn is at practice. He's running drills with his teammates. They are working out hard. Jayvorn is sweating and out of breath.

Around the same time: Jayrode is in the gym at his school playing basketball with his teammates. It doesn't look like he is breaking a sweat as he comes down the court pulling up and shooting a three-pointer and makes it.

Friday mid-afternoon: Jayvorn and Tracy are sitting at a table, eating lunch and working on some class work with their books out laughing and talking.

At about that same time: Jayrode is at the pizza shop at the corner by his school. He is buying pizza for all his friends and Tiffany and her friends who are sitting at another table from him and his friends.

Later that afternoon: Jayvorn is in the gym at practice, running drills and working even harder.

As he wipes the sweat from his head with his shirt, he looks exhausted. He tries to keep up with his teammates who are worn out as well.

At that same time: Jayrode is in the hallway of his school with his friends. Everyone is going and coming from class and they are sweating him as if he was the man of the school.

It is now Saturday and Jayvorn is in the park stretching and warming up as he is waiting for Jayrode. He looks up and sees Jayrode coming into the park with a new sweat suit on and new sneakers.

"Oh, look, was it you? Who was talking about running late and missing practice and all kinds of stuff like that?" Jayvorn asks him as he gives Jayrode a five.

"I know! I know! I'm sorry. I just couldn't find anything to wear," Jayrode says as he drops his bag down and starts to stretch his legs and back as they warm up.

"Nothing to wear! It sure doesn't look like that to me," Jayvorn says looking at his new clothes.

"What this! I told you about how I got this," Jayrode says as he shows his outfit off.

"Yeah, I know you got the hookup with your mom!" Jayvorn says as he puts his arms up in the air and wiggles his two fingers up and down on both hands.

"Oh, you got jokes now!" Jayrode says to him.

"Talking about hookups, what's up with you and Tiffany?" Jayrode asks Jayvorn as they start to run around the park.

"Nothing, why?" Jayvorn asks him.

"Because word around school is she a free agent and you know she been sweating me hard!" Jayrode tells him.

"What? Please, go ahead with all that," Jayvorn says in a serious voice.

"I'm saying yo, word is she drop you like a dead basketball. What's up with all that?" Jayrode asks him.

"What! She didn't drop me. And besides…." Jayvorn answers him getting real serious.

"So what's up, let your boy in on it?" Jayrode asks again.

"Look, it's like this…." Jayvorn says as they came into the park and started their drills. "I call her the other week when I found out I was going to this new school, to tell her all about it. She starts tripping, saying how she is tired of being last in my life and all kinds of stuff like that, Jayvorn tells him as they start to do layups.

"What? What she mean by that?" Jayrode asks him.

"I mean, I can't believe what she said," Jayvorn tells him.

"So what she say?" Jayrode asks him again.

"So this is how it went when I called her," says Jayvorn.

"Hey Tiff, I got some good news," Jayvorn said.

"What's that," Tiffany said all happy.

"I'm getting ready to start a new school," I

told her all excited.

"A new school how is that good news," Tiff said as if she is upset.

"I'm saying this new school will help me get into a better college, then that will get me a better chance to go to the NBA. I'm trying to tell her still excited."

"Yeah, yeah, yeah, that's all I hear from you, playing ball and the NBA... I'm tired of all that what about us?" she asked me in a serious voice. "Come on Tiff, you know how I feel about you. When I make it you know you are going to be right on my arm and by my side all the way!" I told her.

"Yeah, well, I'm tired of playing last to everything. It's you and basketball, then you and practice, then you and Jayrode, and now you going to this new school. It's going to be you and this new school. I'm not going to be fifth on your list. You need to be moving me up the ladder, not down," she told me in a smart voice and now she is angry.

"It's not going to be like that. It's a private school only two hours away. I will be staying home and we can still see each other every other day if you want," I told her thinking it will calm her down.

"What! A private school! Oh, please! Now, you telling me you are going to be out there with all those white preppy girls, No, No, no! Please, I know better than that!", she said to me in a really angry voice as if she wanted to scream at me.

"What you trying to say. You know me better than that!" I said to her and now I am starting to get upset.

60

"Look Jayvorn, what I'm saying is if you love me, the way you say you do, you won't leave me in the random school by myself," she told me in a nice voice.

"So, what, you want me to do? You know if I could I would take you with me," I told her.

"No, that's not what I'm saying! I'm saying Jayvorn you need to get your priorities in order. Then let me know where I stand," she told me in a smart voice.

Now, I'm aggravated and say to her, "Look Tiff, maybe you're right. If you can't stand behind me now what makes me think you will stand behind me when I do make it. Besides, maybe we do need some time apart so I can get my priorities in order like you said!"

Then she had the nerve to bang the phone on me and that was the end of our conversation." Jayvorn tells Jayrode as they finish up the last of their drills.

"Man! No wonder she's been in school trippin', sweating all over me, saying I remind her of you, but better," Jayrode tells him as he takes off his sweat suit jacket and Jayvorn sees his new chain on his neck.

"Yeah, I can see how she would say that, new kicks, new clothes, and now a new chain. You sure ballin'. I thought I was the one with the big break," Jayvorn says to Jayrode as he holds up his chain to admire it.

"What, this old thing? My Mom had this for a long time. She just gave it to me, so I can rock

61

it." Jayrode said to him.

"Now what do you have to do? Jayvorn asks.

"You know what it is, we ask this same question every week before we start," Jayrode tells him.

"Man, I don't think I can do one suicide. I've been running all week and this coach got us doing killer drills. He been working us to death," Jayvorn says as he goes and sits down on the bench.

"Yo what's up with that? I haven't heard from that coach yet?" Jayrode asks as he sits next to Jayvorn.

"I don't know, but what I will do is when I get to school I'll ask him," He tells Jayrode.

"Yeah, definitely, do that! Because you know I can't wait to put my moves down on that floor," Jayrode tells him as he stands up and starts to bounce the ball between his legs.

The Lookout

Monday morning: Coach Davis is in his office. He is working on the itinerary for the next game as Jayvorn walks up and knocks on his door, which is open and he goes in.

"Hey coach, I need to talk to you?" Jayvorn asks the coach.

"Yes. Son have a seat," the coach tells him.

"Coach, I have my dude...." Jayvorn was starting to say as he looked up at the coach's face and the coach funnily looks at him.

"I mean my friend who I work out with all the time and is my partner at my old school basketball team. I was wondering why you haven't called him to play for us too." Jayvorn asks him.

"Excuse me son, I don't understand what you are trying to say?" the coach asks him, looking puzzled.

"Well, the night of the championship game is when you said you saw me play and he was on my team. Jayrode was playing as good as me, so I was wondering why you haven't called him yet?" he asked the coach, looking kind of shocked.

"First of all son, I don't know nothing about him. When I was at that game that night all I saw was you doing your thing. That impressed me," the coach told him.

"But I'm saying in the beginning of the game, he dominated the game!" Jayvorn told him as if he was a little better than him.

63

"Well there it is son. I didn't get to the game until the beginning of the second half of the game so all I saw was you playing, not him," the coach insured him as he was trying to figure out why his friend didn't play.

"Oh, so that would explain it. Because he had to leave at halftime to do something important for his mother," Jayvorn says to the coach as he nods his head.

"Look coach, my boy is good, real good. With him and me on the team we will make this team look like an NBA team. It will be show time, two to the right!" he tells the coach all excited.

"Well hold on now son, if he is that good, I will see what I can do for him," the coach says to him.

"I'm telling you coach with him on the team it's like that and he is that good. We can go the tournament and blow them out," Jayvorn told the coach as he tries to convince him about Jayrode.

"Well look son, there is nothing I can do for him right now because the itinerary is in for this game and we leave on Wednesday. But as soon as we get back I will look into him for you," the coach tells him.

"Ok coach, thanks a lot. Here is his name, number and address," Jayvorn said as he picks up a pen off the coach's desk and writes it on the back of the itinerary.

The Girls Decide

At around the same time of the day, Jayrode is in the hallway of his school, at his locker with two of his teammates, Steffon and David. As they are talking and looking at everyone go to and from class. Jayrode looks up and sees Tiffany walking down the hallway right toward them. Jayrode sees her looking and smiling at him as she gets closer he is thinking how good she looks in that mini-skirt and tight shirt. As she walks right up to him and smiles and winks her eye, she grabs his chain with one finger and says softly in his ear: "We need to talk" as she flirts with him and keeps on walking slowly down the hallway.

"Ok, I will catch you after school," he answers her as if he was the man.

"I'm going to hold you to that," she replies as she swings her hair over her shoulder and looks back at him and keeps on walking down the hallway slowly and switching.

"Man, isn't that Jayvorn's girl"? Steffon asks as he stood on one side of Jayrode and David on the other. Steffon bites on one of his knuckles.

"X-girl!" Jayrode tells them as they watch her walk down the hallway as if she is a sexy runway model.

"Man," David says as he makes a face of pain.

"All fair in love and war," Jayrode says as the three of them stare at her butt switching as she walks down the hallway and into her classroom.

Later that day Jayvorn is in the gym locker room changing getting ready to go home, tired from running so many drills and working hard.

At the end of the day, Jayrode is coming out of the school doors and sees Tiff at the corner of the block. He calls to her and runs to catch up to her. "Hey Tiff, what's up?" he asks as he catches up to her.

"No what's up with you?" she asks him.

"What you mean?" he asks her with a smile.

"You know what I mean. Why are you avoiding me?"; she asks him as she is flirting with him.

"Avoiding you? I'm not avoiding you.", he says to her.

"Yeah, so what's up with you and me?", she asks in a sexy voice.

"What's up is you used to be my boy's girl.", he tells her.

"Oh please, your boy! He got a lot of other bougie white girls on his mind up at the preppy school of his," she tells him with an attitude.

"Come on now, why you're going there about my boy. You know better than that. He's just trying to get things together for himself," he tells her.

"Well, all I know is he hasn't called me, and I'm trying to get things together with you and me," she says as she gets close up on him and feels on his chest.

"So what are you trying to say?", he asks her.

"What I am saying is do you want to come over to my house?", she asks him as she is flirting with him.

"Why, who's there?", he says.

"Nobody," she answers him softly in his ear.

"Shit, Ok, bet! Let's go!" he tells her as he put his arm around her and they walk off to her house.

The next morning Jayvorn and Tracy are at the train station waiting for their train to go to school and laughing and joking around like they always do. They didn't notice Jayrode on the other side of the station watching them with a look of jealousy in his eyes and betrayal on his face. He doesn't say anything to them as he watches their train pull in from one side and his from the other. They get on their train and he got on his. The trains go their separate ways.

Later that day at Clark Men, Jayvorn is at practice running drills with his teammate as the coach blows the whistle. "Ok boys, hit the showers. I will see you tonight at the pep rally," the coach tells them.

Later that night at the pep rally Jayvorn is there with Tracy joking around. He is standing behind her with his arms around her, hugging her. The coach is up on the stage talking to the kids and calling off the names on his itinerary. As they all go up on the stage, everyone cheers them on. The coach got to the end of the list and said: "Now, last but not least, we have a new guy on the team, who is working real hard. I know he will not only take us to the championship but will win it and bring it home to us. So without further ado, I give you Jayvorn Hall! Where are you son?" the coach said as the crowd started cheering and clapping for him. Tracy turns around and hugs and kisses him on the lips. He is shocked because this is the first time she has kissed him. Not like he didn't want to kiss her, but it took him by surprise, the way she did it. It left him stunned.

"There he goes! Come on son, come up here!" the coach tells him on the mic, as everyone guides him to the stage.

The Mix

The next day after school Jayrode is in the park. He is walking back and forth nervously as he waits on Jayvorn. He checks his watch as he looks down the block. He sees Jayvorn running to the park with his black duffel bag on his arm as Jayvorn runs into the park to talk with Jayrode. He drops his black duffel bag right next to Jayrode's black duffel bag.

"What's up man? I'm sorry I'm late," Jayvorn tells him as he gives Jayrode five.

"It's ok because…" Jayrode was saying as Jayvorn interrupts him.

"I just came to tell you, I'm not going to be able to practice today because I have to go to my first basketball tournament today," he told him.

"Oh word! That's good. I'm glad to hear that because I have something that I need to do today, so that worked out for the both of us" Jayrode tells him.

"Yeah, I guess that did. So look, I'm going to the bus depot now and I will be gone for a week and a half, so are you going to be cool with that?" Jayvorn asks him.

"Yo man, don't sweat it. Just don't forget to represent. I will see you next Saturday," Jayrode tells him.

"You know I will, but if not next Saturday definitely next Wednesday," Jayvorn says as he picks up the black duffel bag and starts to run out the park to the train.

"Yo don't forget!" Jayrode yells back to him as he puts up two fingers and pats his chest.

"You know it baby, two to the right," Jayvorn yells back to Jayrode as he makes the same gesture and runs back down the block. Jayrode then picks up the other black duffel bag and goes out of the park the other way.

A few minutes later: Jayrode is walking around the corner with his hoodie on his head, nodding and pretending to play the drum. He is not paying attention as he starts walking down the block where there are some abandoned buildings in the middle of the block.

"We have an unidentified black male heading your way," comes from a van across the street from an abandoned building. It is four cops inside watching Jayrode.

"He has on a black hoody and blue jeans," goes over the radio from the van.

"I got him," a bum says into his shirt as he is laying on some step. He is an undercover cop.

"Does anyone see his face?" comes from the van to the other cops.

"That's a negative, his hoody is covering his face," come from two cops in a parked car down at the end of the block. Jayrode is walking down that way as he passes some of the buildings.

"I didn't get it, he passed me too fast," the cop on the steps says in his shirt.

"Ok, look if he heads into the building, then it's on!" the cop in the van tells everyone over the radio. As Jayrode comes in front of one of the abandoned building, he turns and goes inside.

"It's a go. No one moves until I say so. On my word then, we move in!" comes from the cops in the van.

Jayrode goes up two flights of stairs, then into an abandoned apartment at the end of the hallway, when he sees two guys standing across a table from each other waiting for him. One of the guys looks up with a mad look on his face.

"Yo, Jayrock, where the fuck you been. You know you're late," the guy with the mad look asks him with an angry voice.

"I'm sorry Dee. I had to let my boy know that I was not going to make it to practice today," Jayrode answers Dee as he walks into the apartment.

"Yo, get the hell over here. I told you that damn basketball is going to get your ass in trouble someday. Now, where's my shit?" Dee asks Jayrode as he walks up to the table where Dee is standing on one side and the other guy is on the other side of the table.

"I got it right here Dee," Jayrode told him as he put the black bag on the table. He opened it and reached into the bag. In shock he yells, "Oh shit! It's not my bag it's Jayvorn's!"

"What the fuck do you mean? Where's my shit?" Dee asks him again with a real mean voice as he reaches behind his back.

"Look Dee, my boy Jayvorn got my bag by accident and I got his. He just went to the bus depot to go to a basketball tournament. If I leave now I can probably catch him, or I can get it from him when he gets back," Jayrode tells Dee in a frantic and scared voice looking at Dee puzzled and surprised.

"What!" Dee says real mad, as he clutches tightly to what is in his hand behind him.

"It's a no go! It's a no go! The other guy says into his jacket thinking no one heard or noticed him.

"What the fuck! What you mean it's a no go! What you trying to set me up?" Dee says real mad as he turns and looks at the other guy. (Bang) A gun goes off as Dee pulls it from behind his back and fires it into the guy's head all in one moment. Jayrode is standing there looking at Dee as it happens so fast he doesn't really know what just happened. Jayrode stands there in shock as he looks down at the guy on the floor with blood coming from his head. His jacket is open and Jayrode saw something silver and square sticking out of it.

"You shot him Dee!" Jayrode says as he turns and looks at Dee. Dee points the gun at him.

"Shots fired! Shots fired!" they both hear as Dee looks up and realize the police are coming up the stairs. He grabs Jayrode as Jayrode grabs his bag. Dee pulls him towards a window in the next room.

"Jump!" Dee tells Jayrode as Jayrode looks down and sees a hole in the floor that leads to the apartment beneath them. Jayrode clutches his bag in front of him and Dee pushes him down into the hole. He lands on some mattresses in the apartment below him. He falls back up against the wall. In a minute Dee came down behind him. The cops go up to the apartment on the third floor and see the undercover cop on the floor dead with blood all over the floor. Dee grabs Jayrode and goes out a window onto a fire escape. They jump down and run into an alley behind one of the abandoned buildings. Jayrode is leaning up against a door. Dee turns and faces him and pulls out the gun from his waist and points it at Jayrode.

"Now where's my shit?" Dee asks Jayrode in a real serious voice with the gun pointed at him. Jayrode puts his hands up and explains to Dee:

"Look Dee, my boy Jayvorn got my bag and I got his. He went to a basketball tournament and when he gets back I will get it for you, I promise Dee!"

"Man I ought..." (Bang) Dee turns and lets off another shot as he looks down and sees he just shot a bum who was lying in the alley and just has knocked over a bottle. As Jayrode feels the doorknob behind him, he turns it slowly as Dee turns back and faces him pointing the gun at him.

"Freeze, drop it!" they both hear as two cops at the other end of the alley. They are pointing their guns at Dee. Dee turns around towards them and points his gun at them. (Bang, bang, bang) Three shots rang out as the cops shot Dee and Dee fires a shot at them. At the same time, Jayrode fell into the doorway unnoticed and unseen by the cops as Dee hit's the ground face down. Jayrode lands on some stair as the door closes and locks in front of him. He sat there in the dark, scared, nervous and panicky with his heart beating a hundred miles a minute out of his chest. He hears the doorknob move as he jumps and looks at the door. It's being checked and one of the cops pushes on the door.

"All clear," he hears from one of the cops.

"Yeah, this door is locked too," the other cop says.

As Jayrode sat in the dark staring at the door, not making a sound, quietly he is thinking, whispering to himself, "If they get in here my life is over."

Jayvorn is on the train as it is pulling into the train station. He grabs up his bag. When the door opens, he takes off running down the platform and out of the station. He runs into the bus depot. As he gets into the port authority, he looks around for the bus schedule to see if he can find where and when his bus is leaving from. As he looks up he sees Dispatcher Track 6 at 5:30 pm, Clarks Man Academy. He looks over and sees another sign that says Track 5, 6 pointing down some stairs. He takes off running to the stairs and hears:

"Young man, young man, young man, you forgot your bag!" a lady calls out to him as she catches up to him at the stairs, she hands it to him.

"Thank you, Miss," he tells her as he takes the bag and goes down the stairs.

"Jayvorn, Jayvorn! We are over here son," the coach yells out to him. As Jayvorn gets to the bottom of the stairs, he looks around and sees

74

everyone is already on the bus.

"What took you? We almost left without you," the coach lets him know, as Jayvorn runs over to him outside of the bus.

"I had to let my boy know I was not going to make it to practice," Jayvorn told him.

"Anyway son, put your bag over there and get onto the bus. We have to go," the coach tells him as he points to a pile of bags that are to be loaded under the bus. Jayvorn throws his bag on top of all them and gets on the bus. The coach gets on behind him.

"We all here now?" the assistant coach asked Coach Davis.

"Yes, that's all of us," he answers him as Jayvorn goes towards the back of the bus and finds a seat in the middle of the bus behind the driver. No one is paying attention to what is going on outside the bus. Jayvorn is joking and talking with his teammates as Coach Davis is sitting up front next to the assistant coach and they are talking. No one sees the three cops with a dog outside the bus walking by. As they get next to the pail of bags, the dog tugs the cop to the pail and starts to sniff and bite on the black bag.

"Good boy, what you got there?" the cop asked the dog as the other two cops walk over to him.

"Release," the cop gives the dog a command as he bends down and takes the bag out of the dog's mouth. He passed it to one of the other cops who takes the bag and gets on the bus.

"May I ask whose bag this is?" the cop asks holding up the black bag, as coach Davis looks at him in a puzzling way. No one answers him or hears what he said.

"Excuse me! May I get everyone's attention? Whose bag is this! The cop asks in a loud voice so everyone could hear him. All the boys looked up to see what was going on and got quiet.

"It's mine, why?" Jayvorn asks, as he stood up and started to walk towards the front of the bus.

"I need you to come with me," the cop tells him.

"Excuse me officer, what's this all about?" Coach Davis asks as Jayvorn walks up to the cop and coach Davis.

The cop then takes Jayvorn by the arm and led him off the bus. The cop didn't answer coach Davis as the two of them got off the bus. All the boys are looking at everything that is going on. As they are asking: "What is going on? What's wrong? Where are they taking him? Why are they taking him?"

"Settle down now, settle down! Look you stay here with the boys and go on to the game. I will find out what is going on and I will meet you there later," the coach tells his assistant. He gets off the bus and follows the three cops and Jayvorn. Everyone was looking out the windows as coach Davis was talking to one of the cops trying to find out what is going on. They follow behind Jayvorn and the two cops. One cop has Jayvorn and the bag, the other has the dog. As they walk through the bus depot, they come to a precinct that was in the port authority.

The cop puts Jayvorn in a room with three chairs and a table. Then closes the door and starts to let Coach Davis know what's going on, and he tries to tell Coach Davis why they are doing what they are doing.

"Look, I am responsible for these boys and we were on our way to a basketball tournament," Coach Davis tells the officer as he was about to talk to him.

"And you are?" the cop asks.

"My name is Davis, Coach Carl Davis of Clark's Men Academy," he responds to the cop.

"Well look, Mr. Davis, we have to do this anytime one of our dogs responds like that to anything or anyone. It's just a routine we have to do. It might be nothing at all. The dog might have smelled some food or something in the boy's bag. All we have to do is ask the boy if we can look in the bag. If we don't find nothing. Then you all can be on your way," the cop tells Coach Davis.

"Well, do you mind if I was in the room with him?" coach Davis asked the cop.

"No, it's ok because the boy is a minor and he needs a guardian or parent with him for us to question him," the cop answers Coach Davis.

As he and Coach Davis go to the door that they put Jayvorn in the cop grabs the bag off the desk and they go inside the room. Jayvorn is standing by the desk in the room as he sees Coach Davis and the cop come in.

"What's going on Coach?" Jayvorn asks with a scared voice and a puzzled look on his face.

"I don't know yet son. But just relax and I will handle it," the coach tells him as they step into the room and the cop closes the door behind them. He puts the bag on the table in front of Jayvorn and Coach Davis.

"Now son is this your bag?" the cop asks Jayvorn.

"Yes, it's my bag. Why?" Jayvorn asks the cop.

"Have anyone gave you anything to hold, or have you left your bag unattended at any time while you were in the bus terminal?" the cop asked Jayvorn.

"No!", Jayvorn answers not thinking.

"So, no one put nothing in your bag that you do or don't know of?", the cop asks.

"No, I don't think so.", Jayvorn answers.

"No, you don't know, or no; no one put nothing in your bag?", the cop asks again.

"No; no one put nothing in my bag I just got to the terminal and ran straight to the bus", Jayvorn answers the cop.

"So, you don't mind if I look in your bag now would you son?" the cop asks Jayvorn as another cop comes into the room with them.

"No, go ahead. I don't have nothing, but my change of clothes, a pair of sneakers, and my basketball," Jayvorn answers.

As the cop opens his bag and reaches in, he pulled out the basketball, then some clothes and then a well-packed thick plastic bag, with tape wrapped around it. Jayvorn looks at it in shock as to say: "what's that and where did it come from." The cop put it down on the table as coach Davis looked at it and then at Jayvorn. Then the cop reaches back into the bag and pulls out another wrapped plastic bag. But this one was opened at the corner and white powder coming out of it. Before Jayvorn can say a word, the cop tastes the white powder falling out of the plastic bag and then nods at the other cop, who's standing behind Jayvorn.

He takes him by the arm. "I'm sorry son, but I have to place you under arrest for possession of narcotics," the cop tells Jayvorn.

"What! That's not mine; I don't know where that stuff came from. I'm telling you that's not mine. I never saw that stuff before in my life!" Jayvorn says with a loud voice, still shocked and puzzled as for how that got in his bag. He looks at Coach Davis, shocked and surprised. Coach Davis looks at him and then the stuff on the table.

"Coach, you got to believe me, that's not mines!" Jayvorn tells him as the first cop puts his stuff back in his bag. He then takes the two plastic packages and his bag out of the room. The other cop goes and handcuffs Jayvorn.

"Look, officer may I have a word with him?" Coach Davis asks the cop that was going out the room.

"Yeah we can do that, but make it quick!" he answers as he nods his head again to the other cop behind Jayvorn. As to say: "Give them a few minutes alone." The cop cuffs Jayvorn to the chair and goes out of the room and closes the door.

"Look, Coach you got to believe me, I never had, never seen or, never mess with no drugs. Believe me Coach, just ask my boy. I swear to you Coach, I swear!" Jayvorn tells him in a serious and sad voice, with a scared look on his face, as if he was about to cry.

"Ok son, settle down. You need to tell me everything that happened today." Coach Davis asks in a soft voice.

"Ok Coach, look, after school, I went home and packed my bag. Then I went to the park to tell my boy that I was not going to be able to practice with him this week because I was leaving for my game. Then I ran to the train station and came straight here." Jayvorn tells him scared as he starts to cry.

"Are you sure you didn't leave anything out?"; Coach asks Jayvorn.

"Nothing that I can think of."; Jayvorn tells him.

"Are you sure?"; the coach asks again, trying to make sure he didn't leave anything out.

"Yes, I'm sure. Look Coach, you just got to believe me. I had nothing to do with this. Please, you got to help me!" Jayvorn says scared and nervous as his eyes start to tear up.

"Look son, I'm going to make a few calls and see what I can do. It might not be much. But I promise you this..." the coach tells Jayvorn, giving him a little hope.

"Yes coach," Jayvorn says sadly.

"I will call your parents and tell them what is going on and where to see about you," the coach let him know as the door opens and the cop walks back in.

"Time's up Coach," the cop tells him. As Coach Davis leaves the room, he looks back at Jayvorn.

"Please coach, help me," Jayvorn said in a very soft voice. Tears drop from his eyes as he is begging the coach for his life with one hand and the other handcuffed to the chair, the cop closes the door.

Back at the abandoned building: Jayrode is sitting on the stairs in the dark staring at the door. He is scared to move, as he listens to all the cop radios and them talking right outside the door as if they were right in front of him. He's listening as he can hear two cops talking clearly.

"Who do we have here," one of the cops with a deep voice says.

"We have one of the suspects and a victim who must have been shot by the suspect before the officers shot him," the other cop answers with a high-pitched voice.

"Do you think he is the other suspect?" The first cop asks. Who seems to be the senior cop?

"No, he doesn't fit the description of the guy who went into the building. He must be a vagrant," the second cop says to him.

"So did we find him?" he asks.

"No, we are still looking for him now," the

second cop tells him.

"Do we at least know who he is or what he looks like," the first cop asks.

"Sorry sir, all we know is what he had on," the second cop lets him know.

"So we don't know if he's the shooter for the cop upstairs or not?" he asks him.

"Well, we have the gun. Hopefully, when ballistics comes back this is the gun that shot the cop and he is the guy who did both shootings," the second cop tells him.

"Well keep looking for this unidentified person. When you find him, I want to know so I can talk to him myself," the first cop informs him.

Jayrode listens on the other side of the door as the voices fade away. He just sat there in the dark looking at the door scared to move. He is nervous and panicking as he said softly while thinking: "At any time now they are going to come in here and my life is over," but praying no one does. He sat there quietly not moving.

The door opens, back at the precinct as the cop goes in the room. Jayvorn is sitting there crying. The cop uncuffs him from the chair and starts to pat him down.

"Is there anything in your pockets that is sharp or pointy?" the cop asks as Jayvorn as he cuffs him behind his back. The cop then goes into his front pockets. He pulls out some change and, a few dollars from one pocket and put it on the table. Then his keys and some more change and put it on the table too. He goes into his back pocket and pulls out his wallet. The cop then puts everything into a brown paper bag then takes Jayvorn out of the room. As the cop has Jayvorn by the arm, he starts to tell him his rights.

As they are leaving the room. Jayvorn looks over and sees Coach Davis on the phone talking to someone. He looks to be explaining what was going on. Coach Davis looks up at Jayvorn as the cop takes him through another door, which leads to the bus depot. The cop took Jayvorn through the terminal and put him in the back of a police car. He gets in on the other side and they drive off.

Later that Night

Jayrode comes into his apartment where his mom is up in the kitchen. She hears him come in.

"Hey boy, where have you been? I been looking and worrying about you all day and night. I haven't seen you since you left for school this morning," she says from the kitchen, where she is fixing her something to eat.

"What? Oh yeah, I was just out with some friends of mine," he answers her shocked to see she was still up.

"Boy, you and that Jayvorn. You're going to be the death of me," she tells him as she comes into the living room where he is.

"You want something to eat?" she asks him, as she goes to give him a hug.

"No thanks mom," he answers as she looks at his face. As it is pale and he looks worn out and, nervous as if something was wrong with him.

"What's going on? Are you ok? You don't look so good. You want me to get you something," she asks him in a concerned voice and a worrying look on her face. As she looks at him knowing her son and seeing that there is something wrong with him.

"No, that's ok mom. I just been doing a lot of running and playing basketball, that's all," he answers her as he walks over to his room.

"Are you sure baby?" she asks him again, still in concern about him or what he was doing all day.

"Yeah, I'm just a little tired. I'm going to go in and crash, that's all mom," he tells her as he goes in his room.

"Well ok baby, I'll see you in the morning," she tells him as he closes his room door. She goes back in the kitchen, with a worried look on her face as she wonders what he has been up to.

Jayrode sits on his bed, mumbling, "Three times I could have been shot, three times!" He looks at his desk and sees his Bible. He reaches for it. He goes on his knees and looks down.

At the same time, Jayvorn is being escorted into a cellblock by a corrections officer. He has on an orange jumpsuit. In one hand he has a small brown bag. Under his arm he has his bedroll. They reach an open cell, Jayvorn looks inside. He sees a desk, a toilet, a sink and a bed with a mat folded up. He steps inside as the correction officer walks away. The cell door slides closed (Boom). Jayvorn jumps as he hears it slams behind him. He turns around scared as he realizes all this is real. He puts the bag on the desk and pulls the mat down. He places the bedroll down on the bed and looks over and sees it sitting on the bed. He thinks to himself; someone must have left it here, as he sits on the bed and reaches over for it; a Bible and grabs it.

He gets up, turns and drops to their knees, facing his bed.

At the same time they say, "Lord, what have I done? How did I get here? What did I do to deserve this? Help me, Jesus. I need you now more than ever. Please God get me out of this trouble."

Both boys drop their heads into their Bible, clutching it tightly as tears fall from their eyes.

Thursday Morning

Jayrode is in class doing his class work. His books are out and open as he is writing and listening to everything that is going on.

At the same time Jayvorn is in his cell, sitting at the window reading his Bible. He looks out, thinking of what just happened.

Later that day Jayrode, is at the basketball court by himself shooting the ball around, thinking of all the things that happened in his life.

At the same time Jayvorn is sitting at a window by himself. He is looking out and praying as he is thinking of all the things that happened in his life.

Arraignment

Edd and Clara are in a crowded courtroom. They are waiting for the court officer to bring Jayvorn in the courtroom.

"The state of New York vs. Jayvorn Hall," one of the bailiffs says as another one opens a door on the side of the courtroom. They bring Jayvorn out of the back and stand him next to his lawyer. He looks over and sees his mom and dad. They are looking at him.

"Look how they got my baby, Edd," Clara says as she looked at him in an orange jumpsuit and handcuffed behind his back. As he stands next to his lawyer, he looks back and sees his mom with her hand over her mouth. As she leans on Edd and grabs his arm.

The clerk reads off the charges: "Possession in the first degree, attempt to distribute in the first degree, and attempt to sell in the second degree."

"How does your client plead?" the Judge asks his lawyer, as the clerk hands him the file.

"Not guilty your honor," his lawyer says as he is going through some papers.

"How do the people feel on bail?" the Judge asks the district attorney.

"With the excess of his charges, and the amount of narcotics he had on him at the time, plus where he was apprehended we feel that he be held without bail," the DA says to the Judge.

"Your honor, my client is a good young man

who has never been in trouble with the law. He is in a fine school. He goes to church with his mother and father every week, who he lives with and is here with him today in court. Besides your honor, he was on his way to a school basketball game at the time of his arrest. Just to note, he just received a scholarship to his school. Both his parents do work. They don't make a lot of money, so with that all in mind, we feel that $20,000. Would be sufficient," his lawyer says to the Judge.

"Your honor, this young man was seized with two kilos of cocaine, $20,000 is hardly a thing in this matter," the DA says.

"Ok, ok, no need to get all hostile. I see where this is going. Bail is set at $1 million, 10% cash or bond. Next case," the Judge tells them.

"Your honor…!" his lawyer says to the Judge as he looks up at him.

Jayvorn looks back at his mom and dad. Clara drops her head and starts to cry. Edd shakes his head back and forth with a powerless look on his face as to say where in the world we are going to get that kind of money.

"Look counselor, if your client can get up two kilos, he can get up a $100,000." The judge says to Jayvorn's lawyer as he hands the file to the clerk.

The bailiff takes Jayvorn back into the door he came out of and the clerk calls the next case as Jayvorn's lawyer heads out of the courtroom with Edd and Clara. They get into the hallway and he hands Edd and Clara his business card.

"So what does this mean? How are we going to get up all that money?" Clara asks him in a frantic voice.

"Look, all this is, is a formality. We will go back for a bail reduction in a month or two, so don't worry about the money. Unless you can talk to the school to see if they will help you out." The lawyer tells them.

"So what happens to my son now?" she asks the lawyer.

"Well, we will have a bail reduction like I said. Then three hearings and by that time I will know what the D.A. has and if they want to make Jayvorn some kind of deal," the lawyer tells them.

"A deal, what kind of deal! My son didn't do anything," Edd said with a slightly angry voice.

"Look Mr. Hall, I'm on your side and we have to look at this realistically," the lawyer tells him as they walk down the hallway. He starts to explain what the cops found on Jayvorn and how everything goes.

Time Starts to Set In

A few days later Jayvorn is in his cell. He is looking around and reading all the little saying on the walls. He takes a pen and stands on his bed and writes over the window: (God bless me, protect me, and Take me out of this place, Jayvorn Hall).

The next day, Jayvorn comes into the visiting room. He sees his mom and dad, and Deacon Brown. They are all so happy to see him as they give him hugs and kisses. Then they all sit down to talk. They are telling Jayvorn how they are working so hard to get him out and get the money for his bail and what the lawyer told them.

The following Wednesday morning: Jayvorn is leaving the visiting room from seeing his mom and dad. As he goes out he looks back and sees his mom starting to cry as his dad holds her in his arms.

The Bad News

Later that same day after school Jayrode is in the park walking back and forth. He is nervous because he knows that Jayvorn is going to be mad at him for what he found in his bag. He is thinking of what to say to Jayvorn or if he got in trouble. He looks at his watch to check the time then sit on the bench.

As he practices his apology and what he is going to say to Jayvorn as soon as he sees him: "Look Jayvorn, I know what you found and believe me I am so, so sorry. I will never let that happen again. It's not like I was selling it or using it. I just picked it up and dropped it off for this guy where ever he wanted it, that's all. Besides, I'm definitely not going to do it no more, after what I went through last week. If you threw it away, good. If not, we can get rid of it now," he says to himself as he looks at his watch again and out the park to see if he can see Jayvorn coming.

An hour goes by and he is nowhere to be seen.

Two hours later Jayrode is outside Jayvorn's house. He is nervous as he goes and knocks on the door. He is scared of what Jayvorn is going to say. Edd is in the kitchen and Clara is in Jayvorn's room. She is holding a school picture of Jayrode and Jayvorn playing basketball as she sat on the bed rocking back and forth with tears in her eyes praying and asking God why is all this happening to her baby.

"I got it baby," Edd says to Clara. As he hears the knock on the door.

"Who is it?" he asks as he got to the door.

"It's me, Jayrode," he hears on the other side of the door. Edd then opens the door.

"Hey son, how are you doing?" he asks Jayrode.

"I'm ok, is Jayvorn home?" he asks Edd, with a scared look on his face.

"Who is it Edd?" Clara asks him with a muffled and cracked voice as if she was crying and you can tell.

"It's Jayrode, Clara," Edd answers her as he stands in the doorway with Jayrode.

"I'll be right there," she tells him.

"No son, haven't you heard?" Edd asks Jayrode.

"Heard what?" Jayrode answers and asks Edd as he stands in the doorway.

"Jayvorn is in jail. He has been there for two weeks now," Edd tells him.

"In jail, what jail! For what?" Jayrode asks him with a shocking voice and a puzzling look on his face.

"Look son now is not a good time. We just came back from seeing him and my wife is a little upset. If you come back in a few days, I will let you know everything," Edd tells him as he starts to close the door.

"Ok sir," Jayrode says to Edd as he took a few steps back and watches Edd close the door in

93

front of him and locks it. Jayrode leans up against the wall and he looks at the door. He hears Clara's voice.

"Edd, where is Jayrode?" she asks him while coming out of Jayvorn's room and down the hallway to the door next to Edd.

"He's gone Clara," Edd tells her as he goes to give her a hug and hold her.

"No!" she cries out as she lies in Edd's arms on his chest.

"Why! Why! Why you let him go Edd, why you let him go. He is the only son I have left out here." she cries out to Edd in his arms as she finally breaks down crying.

"I know baby, I know, it's going to be ok! Believe me baby it's going to be ok," Edd tells her as he holds her in his arms and rubs her back. As Jayrode listens to them outside of the door, he slides down the wall and looks up. He starts to cry and pray: "What have I done, God, what have I done. Just tell me what to do and I will do it. I will make it right, I swear I will make it right," he says to himself in a low voice, as tears fall down from his eyes and face, as he sits on the floor outside the door, looking at it.

The Setback

A few days later Coach Davis is in his office as one of the board members come to his office.

"Hey Carl, can I have a word with you?" he asks as he goes into his office and closes the door.

"Yeah, sure," Coach Davis says as he and the board member takes a seat.

"Look, I talked with the board. We felt that we need to step back from this one," he tells Carl.

"What are you trying to say?" Coach asks in a confusing voice.

"Well look, the school don't need this kind of publicity," he tells the coach.

"Oh, so we just going to leave this kid out to dry?" the coach asks as he starts to get upset.

"It's not like that. All I'm saying is we don't know this kid or anything about him," he tells the coach.

"I know he is a good kid," Coach tells him in a straightforward voice.

"Look, it's not like he has been here since his freshman year. He just came to us this year," he tells Coach.

"Oh, so since he's not an alumnus we can't do anything for him. That's what you are saying?" Coach Davis asks him.

"No that's not what I'm saying," he tells Coach Davis.

"So what are you saying Paul?" Carl asks

him as serious as he can get without going off on him.

"No, what the board is saying, we think that it will be best if we all step back from this one," Paul tells the coach as if it was a warning.

"So when you say we, that means me too?" the Coach asks him.

"Well yes, you are part of this staff." Paul assures him as he gets up and starts out the door.

"Yeah, you right," Carl said to Paul as Paul goes out the office and closes the door behind him. Coach Davis just sits there shaking his head side to side. He can't believe what just happened.

The Playoffs

A few months later it's at the end of the basketball tournament. There are two sportscasters talking. As Jayrode and his team are warming up, they are at Madison Square Gardens for the playoff games.

"Well here we are at the high school playoffs. You know the winner of this will go on and play for the championship Pat?" one of the announcers asks.

"Yes, I do, and what a game we will have this week with all these high school teams Steve," Pat says.

"As you can see it's full of excitement here at the Garden," Steve says.

"Well Steve, you are right. Because it's win or go home for these young men," Pat says.

"Talking about going home, what do you think about King High School? You know this is their first time at the big show?" Steve asks Pat.

"Well for what I hear, they have a young man who is pretty good and has been scoring high numbers for King," Pat tells him.

"Well, I don't know if he can keep it up here. There is a lot of veteran teams here who play hard and for a team that never been here, they don't know what to expect of these other teams on the floor," Steve tells pat.

"Well, you can be right on that Steve. But they say this young man, named Jayrode Spencer.

He is no stranger to hard work. They say he can hold his own on any floor," Pat tells him.

"So what do you think about him? Do you think we will see him in the N.B.A. someday?" Steve asks him.

"Ha! Ha! Ha! Hold Steve, N.B.A, slow down. He has to get through college first. That's the thing a lot of schools like King don't get this far, so most good colleges don't even know who these shining stars or should I say real talented kids are and that is sad," Pat tells Steve.

"Yes, you are right, Pat. So if Jayrode want to be picked up by any of the college scouts he will have to play hard and outshine everyone," Steve says to Pat.

"I don't know about outshining everyone, but I do know he has to play hard. So we will be in for a treat," Pat says to him.

"Well we will see won't we? Only if they can stay in it, and not get knocked out fast," Steve says as the games get underway.

Jayrode dominated each and every game. He scored 29 points in the first game with his team winning 78 to 56.

At the same time Jayvorn is in the jail gym playing ball with some guys. He scored fourteen and his team wins 32 to 12.

In second game, Jayrode scores 33 points and his team wins 86 to 72.

Back at the jail there Jayvorn plays a second game and scores ten points with his team winning 32 to 14.

Jayrode really takes control in the third game scoring 42 points. His team wins by forty points with a final score of 88 to 48.

There was another game played at the jail where Jayvorn scored 12 points and his team wins 32 to 16. In the championship game, Jayrode really explodes. It was as if he was all over the court. There was no stopping him as he scored 55 points and won it all for King. Taking home the trophy with the game winning score of 110 to 70. Never has a high school playoff game scored so high. It was as if you were at the NBA as everyone was going wild after the game.

In the last game Jayvorn goes off scoring eighteen points and winning it just befreo the CO call them in from the gym. The score was 32 to 8 everyone was going off and cheering as they went back to their cell block.

As Jayvorn, and Jayrode are playing their games you can tell both of them are doing the same moves and winning as if they were in the same game, playing the same game , the same way, inseparable.

At the prison gym, the C.O. calls the prisoners in. Jayvorn puts the basketball down. The inmates cheer him as they go back to their cells.

A few months later Coach Davis is in his office, reading an envelope that he just got. He opens it and starts to read the letter. As he reads it he picks up the phone and makes a call.

"Fordham University, Jernay speaking how may I help you?" She says on the other end of the phone.

"Yes, may I speak with Mr. Wilson please?" Coach Davis asks her.

"Hold on please. May I ask who's calling?" Jernay asks.

"Yes, my name is Coach Carl Davis."; he answered.

"One moment please."; she lets him know.

As Coach Davis is hold the phone he is reading the letter trying to figure out what it means.

"Hey Carl," Mr. Wilson says as he gets on the phone.

"Hey Phil, I got your letter and I don't really understand what you mean by it?" Carl asks him.

"Well Carl, what it is, your application was accepted but it's for the assistant coach's job. That is only because Coach Strong is going to retire in a year or two. At that time we will move you up to head coach. Are you ok with that?" Phil asks him.

"Well yeah, that will be fine," Carl tells him.

"Ok then, glad to have you on board. So I will see you at the beginning of the school year." Phil lets him know in a cheerful voice.

"Yes you will, and I'm glad to be on board," Coach Davis says and then hangs up the phone.

Coach Davis then looks over at a box next to the wall. He goes and picks it up and then comes back to his desk. As he starts to pack the box with some of his papers and things, without noticing it he picks up some papers with the itinerary that has Jayrode's name, number, and information on the back of it. He puts it on top of all his stuff in the box and goes out the door.

New Live, New Changes

A month later Jayrode is getting off the elevator in his building on his floor. He is going through his mail he has in his hand. He sees a letter addressed to him from Penn State University. At the same time, he looks up and sees Tiffany at his apartment door. He looks at her and sees she has on a blue baggy dress. She is looking really good to him right about now.

"Hey, what's up Tiff? I haven't seen you in school or nowhere in the last few months," he says to her, as he walks down the hallway from the elevator to his apartment door where she is standing, as he opens the letter. "So what's up? Where have you been?" he asks her as he is still looking at the letter and paying her very little attention to her.

"That's what I need to talk to you about," she tells him in a serious voice, as he goes to the door and unlocks it.

"Ok, come in, you know my mom's not home," he tells her as if he had other things on his mind like fooling around as he opens the door.

"Boy please!" she says to him with her lips twisted up, looking at him as if he is real stupid, as they go inside the apartment.

"Jayrode I really need to talk to you," she tells him as he is starting to read his letter.

"Go ahead, I'm listening," he says as he is still reading the letter.

"No, I need you to pay attention to me!" she

says with a very serious voice.

"Go ahead, just tell me what it is," he says still reading the letter.

"Look boy, I'm pregnant!" she says with her eyes wide open and her lips twisted up in a mad voice, because he's not paying her no mind. "And it's yours!"

"What!" he says loudly as he drops his arms by his side and looks at her. "Pregnant, are you sure?" he asks her looking puzzled.

"Yes. Can't you see," she says as she pulls on the sides of her dress to show him her stomach.

"I'm saying, is it mines?", he asks her looking confused.

"Yes, it's yours. I'm not that type of girl. I know who I been with and besides I don't sleep around," she tells him in a disgusted voice, as to say why would you even say or ask that question.

"But I'm saying what about...." he starts to ask as he shakes his head side to side.

"Please don't go there. I never been with that boy," she tells him, looking at him as if to say I don't believe you. Stopping him before he ever finishes his sentence.

"So what do this mean?" he asks her with a real stupid look on his face.

"It means you're going to be a daddy," she tells him as she looks at him with a serious look on her face as she says. "You sound as stupid as you look."

"A baby! I can't be no daddy, I'm going to college," he said to her as he looks at her as to say this can't be happening to me now!

"What? Excuse me?!"; she says looking at him as to say boy don't even play with me.

"That's what this letter I just got says. I got a full scholarship to Penn State," he tells her as he shows her the letter in his hand.

"So what does that have to do with me?" she asks him, looking at him pointing at the letter.

"Look, Tiff..." he says as he falls down on his knees, holding her by the waist and rubbing her stomach. "If you let me go to college, I promise you when I get out and go to the N.B.A., I will marry you, I swear on it!" he tells her as he looks up at her on his knees rubbing her stomach.

"What if you don't go to the N.B.A.?" she asks him as she looks down at him straight in his eyes.

"Come on now! You know how good I play. Besides even if I don't make it, I will still marry you the day after I graduate," he tells her as he is on his knees rubbing her stomach.

"You promise Jayrode?"; she asks looking down at him on his knees.

"I swear!"; he answers her looking up at her.

"Well ok, I won't say nothing to no one or bother you. But you're going to have to help me while you're in school."; she lets him know with a serious look in her eyes.

"No problem, I will get a job. Send you money, come see you and you can come see me every chance we get," he tells her.

"I'm going to hold you to that," she tells him

as she pushes his hand off her stomach.

"I promise Tiff!" he tells her as he looks up at her.

"Ok then, now boy get off your knees...." she says looking at him as if he was crazy, "No, matter of fact stay down there, you need to beg me a little more," she tells him as she smiles at him.

The Beginning to the End

Around the same time Edd and Clara are at Jayvorn lawyer's office, as they are sitting in the reception area waiting to see Jayvorn's lawyer.

"Come this way please," the receptionist says to them, as she walks to the back and they follow her to a conference room where Jayvorn's lawyer is sitting with Jayvorn's case spread out in front of him.

"How are you all doing, Mr. and Mrs. Hall," he says to them as he stands up and stretches out his hand to greet them.

"We are as fine as we can be," Edd tells him, as he and Clara go into the room. Edd shakes the lawyer's hand.

"Ok then, please have a seat, and we can get right down to it," he tells them as he pulls out a seat for Clara.

"So, Mr. Tanner, what's going on with my son's case? When will he get out of that place?" Clara asks him with a concerned voice, as her and Edd sat down at the table and sees all the papers.

"Well, Mr. and Mrs. Hall I'm not going to beat around the bush with you. Like I explained to you before, yes, we done went through all the hearings and everything, now the D.A. has made a very good offer," he tells them as he sits down and goes through the papers in Jayvorn's case.

"What do you mean an offer? My son hasn't done anything!" Edd tells him in an angry voice.

"Why they haven't found who put this stuff in my son's bag?" he finishes saying as he is looking at Mr. Tanner.

"Look Mr. Hall, I'm on your side. But here is what the D.A. has on your son Jayvorn," he tells them as he hands Edd some papers to read.

"So what is all this?" Clara asks him as Edd try to understand the papers.

"Well Mrs. Hall, this is the D.A. discovery and the indictment they have on Jayvorn," he tells her.

"Well, what is this here?" Edd asks as he hands one of the papers back to Mr. Tanner.

"Hold on! We will go through everything that is in your son's case, so we won't have to keep going back and forth over every other thing," Mr. Tanner says as he flips open his copy of Jayvorn's case, as Edd and Clara look over theirs.

"This is the discovery from the lab. It shows when Jayvorn was arrested; he had 4.4 pounds of cocaine in his bag. Now this is the statement of the officers where they testified that they ask Jayvorn if the bag was his and if he left it unattended at any time and if anyone gave him anything to hold or did he have anything in his bag that was not his..." he was saying as Clara stops him and says "Yes, them drugs," with her face all serious.

"I understand what you are trying to say Mrs. Hall but let me finish," Mr. Tanner tells her. "Now then, Jayvorn answers no to everything. He said no he didn't leave his bag, no, no one gave him nothing to hold, and no, no one put nothing in his bag. So at that time they ask if they can search his bag in front of another officer and his gym teacher who was in the room at the time of them questioning him. He then pulls out his basketball, some clothes, which Jayvorn said was in his bag. Then two well wrapped plastic packages. One was open at the corner. The cop then said he saw what looked like white powder coming out of it. At that time the officer said he taste it and saw that it was indeed narcotics," Mr. Tanner tells them as he reads the officer's statement from the indictment.

"So tell me this. How did they get my son's bag in the first place? How did they know it was his or what was in it?" Edd asks Mr. Tanner.

"I'm getting to that now," Mr. Tanner tells him. "Officer Hunter states; "On a routine walkthrough with his police dog when they secured a black duffle bag on a pile of luggage being loaded on a bus."

"So is there anything you can do to get my son out of this mess. I know we don't have much money, but we will give you everything we have," Edd tells Mr. Tanner with a sad and concerned voice, as he looks at Clara and sees her about to cry, then back at Mr. Tanner.

"Look Mr. Hall, it doesn't matter how much money you pay me. I still will give your son Jayvorn the best defense he's going to get out there. If it was up to me, looking at everything, I would say take the deal the D.A. is offering but it is not; it's up to Jayvorn. When I talked to him about the deal the D.A. was offering, he said; "I will do whatever my mom and dad wants to do," so that means it is up to you too," Mr. Tanner tells them.

"So what is this deal?" Clara asks as she holds Edd's hand.

"Well, the D.A. said if he pleaded out now they will offer him twenty years, but if we go to trial he can get thirty to forty-five years. That is ten to fifteen years for each count. That is what he is looking at," Mr. Tanner informs them about.

"Twenty years! That's not a deal, that's a lifetime!" Edd says in shock as Clara puts her hand over her mouth as she gasps for air.

"Well, if we go to trial and lose, he can get forty-five years to life. Now, it is going to take a miracle to win this one with all the evidence stacked against him. We are going to need a prayer or someone to step up and say this stuff is theirs or they saw someone put it in his bag," Mr. Tanner tells them as he looks at Clara.

"Those two words you just said, Mr. Tanner, are the key words, because I know that my Father, Lord, and Savior, Jesus will see my son through this," Clara tells him with a strong and straight face, as she looks at Mr. Tanner and her voice is filled with faith and belief.

"Well, since you feel that strongly, I do have to ask do you know a Jayrode?" Mr. Tanner asks as Clara is whipping her face from the tears she had before. Edd looks up at Mr. Tanner.

"Yes we do! What does he have to do with this?" Edd asks with a puzzled look on his face as both Clara and Edd look at Mr. Tanner to see what he was going to say.

"Well it might be nothing and it might help with everything, because Jayvorn keeps asking me to talk with him. He might can tell me who or if anyone put something in his bag. Because when he was in the park to see Jayrode, before he went to the bus, this is one of two times he put his bag down and it was out of his sight," Mr. Tanner tells them as he looks over his notes he had wrote when he was talking to Jayvorn.

"You said one of the two times? What is the other time?" Clara asks Mr. Tanner.

"Well, when Jayvorn got into the bus terminal he said he stopped to look at the itinerary he put his bag down. When he saw what time and where the bus was pulling out from, he ran to the stairs, that's when he heard a white lady calling him and came running behind him. She gave him back his bag at that time," Mr. Tanner tells Clara.

"So maybe that's when someone could have put the drugs in his bag," Clara asks with a little sign of hope.

"I don't know but like you said, a prayer and a miracle," Mr. Tanner said to them, as he finished telling them how he is going to defend Jayvorn.

The Other Lookout

Later that same day: Cindy is coming in to her apartment. As she opens the door, the phone starts to ring. She goes into the kitchen to put her bags down, from where she had gone food shopping. She then picks up the kitchen phone that is on the wall.

"Speaking," Cindy says as she answers the phone, while she is putting her bags down on the counter.

"Hey Cindy! How are you doing girl?" Clara asks her in a sad voice on the other end of the phone.

"No! How are you doing girl? Are you ok?" Cindy asks her in a concerned voice.

"Not so good girl. We just came back from seeing Jayvorn's lawyer," Clara tells her.

"I heard. I'm so sorry. I know I haven't come out to see you and everything, but with this new job girl, I don't have time to do nothing but work and sleep. So how is my baby boy doing in there? Is he holding his head up in there?" Cindy asks her as she starts to unpack the food out of her bags.

"Yeah, he's doing ok. We go to see him every chance we get," Clara tells her.

"You need to let me know the next time you go to see him, so I can check my schedule and we will go with you," Cindy tells her while she is putting her food away. She turns to the refrigerator and sees the letter from Penn State. It's for Jayrode and she starts to read it as if he just put it there so she can see it.

"Well, whenever you get a day off, you can call me. We can go see him together. I know he would love to see you, especially Jayrode," she tells her.

"You know you are so right Clara, because I know Jayrode would love to see him too," Cindy tells her as she takes the letter off the refrigerator and finishes reading it.

"Well Cindy, is Jayrode there? Can I talk with him?" Clara asks her

"No, he's not. He hasn't got in yet," Cindy tells her as she got the letter in her hand reading it.

"Well, when he comes in can you tell him to call me? I really need to talk to him," Clara asks her.

"Sure girl, what's going on?" Cindy asks her.

"Well girl, it might be nothing, but then again it might be everything we are praying for," Clara tells her.

"Yeah, what is that?" she asks trying to find out what it is all puzzled.

"Well the lawyer told us that Jayvorn said Jayrode might know who or how that stuff got in his bag. He said that the day he left for the bus, he had stopped in the park and saw Jayrode. I guess he had put his bag down and he wanted to know if Jayrode know or seen, if anyone was near his bag or put something in his bag or looking for a bag like his bag, or anything like that," Clara let her know.

"Well girl, as soon as he comes in I will sure enough ask him. If he does know something I will call you myself," she lets Clara know as if she was concerned.

"Ok, Cindy, thank you girl," Clara tells her.

"No problem girl and hold your head up, God will work it out. I will keep you in my prayers," Cindy tells Clara as she is thinking about the other night when Jayrode came in late.

"Thank you, I sure enough need it," Clara lets her know.

"Ok girl, talk to you later," Cindy tells Clara as she hears Jayrode coming in.

"Ok girl, later," Clara says as she hangs up the phone.

"Hey mom, who was that?" Jayrode asks as he comes in the kitchen and sees his mom hanging up the phone.

"Oh that was just Mrs. Clara. She was telling me how everything was going with Jayvorn and his case, she tells him with a sad look on her face.

"Oh yeah, how is he doing?" he asks all concerned and excited.

"He's doing ok in there," she tells him as she puts her hands behind her back to try to hide the letter she was reading.

"So when's he coming home?" he asks his mom not paying any attention to his mother or what she is doing.

"They don't know, but not for a long time. It just doesn't look so good for him, but enough about that bad news. Let's talk about this good news," she tells him all excited as she pulls the letter from behind her back.

"My baby's going to college, he's going to college, he's going to college," she starts to sing as she does a dance in front of him. She hugs and kisses him.

"Hold on! Hold on! I know mom. I put it there so you could see it," he tells her as he pulls back from her. He watches her do her shimmy dance. He starts to laugh and smile at her.

"Mom, if you think that is good news, wait until you hear this," he tells her as she is all happy and excited.

"Hear what?" she asks him with a big smile on her face.

"I got some more kind of good news and some good news for you," he tells her, with his eyebrows lifted and a funny grin on his face.

"What kind of good news, and good news you got for me? Besides you going to college?" she asks him as she looks at the paper in her hand, then looks back at his stupid look on his face.

"Well, I'm going to be a daddy!" he tells her with a big smile on his face and his arms wide open as to say surprise.

"What!" she shouts as she looks at him with that evil mother arched eyebrow look.

"A daddy! What you mean a daddy? And by who?" she asks him as her mood, face, voice and, look changes to that upset serious mother attitude.

"You know my girl Tiffany, mom," he said

with a big smile as he is happy to be a daddy.

"Oh no, not that little heifer! Didn't she use to go out with Jayvorn? And how do you know she is pregnant?" she asks as she starts to wind up to go off on him.

"Yeah, she used to go with him, but they been broke up. Yes, she is pregnant. She came by last week to tell me and I seen her stomach," he tells her still smiling.

"Well how do you know it's yours?" she asks him.

"Mom!" he says.

"Well do you? When that baby is born we are going to get some tests done and you will see. No! I'm going to make sure it's your baby! Besides you are going to college. Ain't no heifer going to mess up my baby's life, no not anyone!" she tells him as she starts to go off.

"That's what I'm trying to tell you mom," he says still smiling.

"Boy you know better! Now get that smile off your face, before I knock it off. Now what are you trying to tell me?" she asks him in a really snotty and upsetting way, holding her hand with the letter up and back as if she is going to hit him right in the head.

"Look mom, me and Tiff, we talk…." he was telling her as she interrupts him.

"Ah, I'm listening!" she says in a smart way with her lips twisted up as she leans back up against the refrigerator and begins to pat her feet.

"She said she will let me go to college. She

won't sweat me or bother me too much. She's not going to say nothing to no one and she is going to take care of the baby and everything while I'm in school. I agreed to help her with the baby as much as possible. I will get a part- time job out there. I will send her money and everything. When I'm not in school or playing ball I can come up here or she can come out there to see me. After I graduate we will get married," he tells his mom.

"Oh, so you two just got it all planned out huh? But let me tell you something boy, Mr. Jayrode Spencer! If that baby is yours and we will find out and if that girl does everything that she says, you better hold yourself to your word, because look at me. I'm your mother and I know how hard it is raising a baby by yourself. That girl is young, and she got a hard road in front of her. I'm telling you boy, you better do what you say!" she tells him as she looks him dead in the eyes with a real serious face that says I'm not playing.

"Yes mom I am! Because I don't want my baby to grow up without a dad, like I did," he tells his mom as he looks her straight in her eyes, without a smile and a serious face.

"I can't believe this boy. Making me a grandma all ready and I'm not even forty yet. Hell, I'm nowhere near my late thirties. I should have just knocked that smile right off his face. Shit, I don't know who they think they are. Talking about they got everything planned out!" she says out loud to herself rambling as she walks out of the kitchen and to her room. Jayrode stands there watching her go off going into her room.

"And I'm not babysitting, so don't bring that baby to my house!" she yells back at him as she slams her room door. Jayrode just stands there listening to her go off and ramble on in her room as he is laughing and smiling. "And I'm not a grandma so she bet not call me that," she yells back at him through the door.

Waiting for the Time to Begin

A few days later Jayvorn is in the courtroom sitting next to his lawyer as the bailiff say to him, "Please rise." He takes a paper from the head juror and passes it to the judge, Jayvorn stands and looks behind him. He sees his pastor and Tracy, who is sitting in the back by herself crying. She is holding her head down. Jayvorn keeps turning his head behind him as if he was looking for someone other than his family and friends who were there with him through the whole trial.

"What's going on Jayvorn? You have been looking back through the whole trial. Are you ok?" his lawyer asks him as he taps Jayvorn on the arm.

"Yeah, I'm ok. I am just looking for someone to show up that's all," Jayvorn said to his lawyer as he turns and looks at the judge. The judge reads the paper and hands it back to the bailiff. The bailiff takes the paper and hands it back to the head juror who is standing up.

"How do you find?" the judge asks the head juror.

"We find the defendant guilty of all charges."; the head juror says as he reads off the paper and sits back down.

"Oh my God no! Not my baby. Don't take my baby from me," Clara cries out as she breaks down and cries on Edd's shoulder. Edd reaches out to Jayvorn and hugs him.

"Son it will be ok. We will never stop

fighting for you," Edd tells him as everyone starts to yell and cry as they get mad.

"No, you got the wrong one. He didn't do anything. He's a good boy. I can't believe this!" everyone was crying out.

"Order in the court, order in the court," the judge says as he bangs his gavel.

"Bailiff, remove the jury," he tells the bailiff. As the twelve jurors leave the stand, the bailiff leads them through a side door. Everyone sits back down as Jayvorn and his lawyer is the only two standing.

"By order of this court, I remand you to the custody of the Sheriff's Department until such time within the next sixty days, that you are so ordered to appear before this court for sentencing," the judge says to Jayvorn and his lawyer.

As the court officer takes Jayvorn by the arm and leads him out of the courtroom, Clara starts to cry as everyone stands back up. His lawyer walks over to talk with Edd and Clara. The deacon and the pastor come to console them as Coach Davis is standing off to the side.

"So what happens now?" Clara asks with tears falling from her face as she is crying.

"Well now you need to have everyone you know to write letters in Jayvorn's behalf, and then get them to me so I can get them all together for the judge. We need to hope and pray he has mercy on Jayvorn and don't sentence him harshly," Mr. Tanner tells them as they start to walk out of the courtroom. As they walk past Coach Davis, Edd stops and looks at him.

"And you said he made the best choice of his life. I know I should not have let my son go to your school," Edd tells him as he looks at Coach Davis with a look of disgust, then turns and consoles his wife. As they all walk out of the courtroom, Coach Davis sits back down and drops his head in his hands and starts to cry. He shakes his head and says to himself, "No, I can't believe this young man's life is all over with."

Two months later Jayrode is in his room. He is packing his things up for college. He looks up on his desk and sees his bus ticket. As he starts to smile he goes over to his calendar and marks off one day.

"Two more days to go," he says to himself as he looks back at the ticket and the letter from Penn State. At that time the phone rings and he goes in the living room and answers it.

"Hello, speak to me," he said as he picks it up.

"Jayrode, it's time! I need you now!" comes from the other end of the phone, as he looks at the phone and notices Tiff's voice. He hangs up and grabs up his keys that are next to the phone and runs out the door...

Jayrode is in the waiting room with his mother and Tiffany's parents. The doctor comes in. "It's a healthy baby boy," the doctor tells them as Jayrode jumps up with tears in his eyes.

"Yes! Yes!" Jayrode shouts as they all jump up and go to the doctor.

"Can we see the baby?" Cindy asks all

120

excited.

"Yes, how is our daughter?" Tiffany's mom asks the doctor, also happy.

"Yes, your daughter is fine, and you can see the baby as soon as they get him all cleaned up," the doctor tells them as she goes out of the room, leaving them all so happy.

The same day and time Jayvorn is in the courtroom. He is standing beside his lawyer in front of the judge. He is waiting to hear his sentence as he looks around only to see his mom and dad there with him.

"I look over and read all the recommendations and hear the testimony of your mom and dad. I took all this into consideration. I see son that you are a good and fine young man who just got caught up in the wrong doing so looking at your age at the time of your arrest, to now at the time you are here before me. At this time of your sentencing, I see you have just became an adult and so I am taking that into consideration as well, as I impose my sentence," the judge says. As Jayvorn looks up at him with teary watery eyes, Edd is holding Clara who is sitting right behind Jayvorn and his lawyer. She holds Edd's hand and begins to pray that the judge doesn't give her son a lot of time.

The judge looks down at Jayvorn.

"So with all that I just told you, I hereby sentence you to 360 months, to be served at a state minimum facility," the judge says, as Jayvorn looks at his lawyer and drops his head with tears coming from his eyes.

"No! No! No! Not my baby. Don't take him from me," Clara cries out as she jumps up and reaches out for Jayvorn. Ed sits back in shock as he looks at his hand trying to count how many years that is, as the bailiff takes Jayvorn out of the courtroom.

En Route

Two days later Jayrode is at the bus terminal, on the line waiting to get on the bus marked Pennsylvania. As he starts to get on the bus he hands his ticket to the bus driver.

"So where are you heading to?" a guy behind him asks.

"Penn State," Jayrode tells him as he gets on the bus, all happy and smiling. He takes a seat in the middle of the bus behind the driver near the window.

Jayvorn is in a holding cell on a line, shackled up waiting to get on the bus that marked Down State. As the guards starts to move everyone out to get on the bus, he looks back at the inmate behind him. "Yo! Where are we going now?" Jayvorn asks him.

"We are going Down State to get a number, and then to the facility you will be doing your time at," the inmate tells him.

Jayvorn takes a seat in the middle of the bus behind the driver next to the window.

Jayrode has now arrived on campus and is walking around the campus looking at everything. He is amazed at how big and beautiful everything is as he reaches his dorm and he is getting unpacked he shakes his head and smiles.

Jayvorn is getting off the bus and looks at everything in fear of how big and scary everything is. He arrives at his cell and is now fixing up his bed as he looks around and shakes his head in fear.

A few days have passed and Jayrode is at the dorm hall. He is getting his classes and meeting his professors.

While Jayvorn is in the chapel hall meeting the warden and all the staff, as they go over all the rules.

As time goes by Jayrode walks around campus with his books trying to find all his classes.

Jayvorn is walking around meeting other inmates from where he lives, and he finds out where everything is and how everything goes so he can get settled in to do his time.

An Offering

One year later Deacon Brown is sitting in the visiting room. He is waiting on Jayvorn to come out so they can talk. As Jayvorn comes in to the visiting room he looks around and sees all the other inmates and their families. He is looking for his mom and dad, but all he sees is Deacon Brown sitting by himself in a corner. As Jayvorn walks over to the table and sits on the other side. He looks at Deacon Brown with a funny and puzzling look.

"Where's my mom and dad?" he asks Deacon Brown as he is shocked to see him.

"They're not here this time son. They asked me to come up and talk with you," Deacon Brown tells him.

"Why, what's this about?" he asks trying to figure out what is going on.

"Well son, your mom feels that you might need some prayer and guidance over your life. They say son that you are losing your faith in the Lord. Do you want to tell me about it?" Deacon Brown asks him as he looks at him across the table.

"What! What are you talking about Coach?" Jayvorn asks him as he starts to get upset.

"Look son, they tell me the last time they were here it looked as if you were angry and running away from God."; Deacon Brown informs him.

"Angry huh! Yeah, I'm angry with God!" Jayvorn says with a loud voice as he gets hostile with what the coach just told him.

"Calm down son!" Deacon Brown tells him as he looks around and sees everyone looking at them.

"Calm down, Coach, please! I can't believe you came all the way up here just to talk to me about God and faith because if God was there I wouldn't be here and faith, please. I had faith in Him all the way through my trial and you know what that got me, thirty years, huh! And believe, yeah, I believe in him. Just like I believe in the fact that the only one person that could have got me out of this mess would have walked into that courtroom and when I looked around for him, he was nowhere to be found and never was God. But the funny thing Coach is I saw everyone there but them two! I saw my mom, my dad, the pastor, you, my other coach, and members from the church and even a girl I just met in school. Her name's Tracy. I saw everyone but the two people I needed the most, God and my best friend. So please Coach, don't be coming here asking, or talking, or telling me about God, faith or anything in that manner. You know what, as a matter of fact, this visit is over."; he tells Deacon Brown as he jumps up out of his angry with blood fire red eyes.

Jayvorn jumps up out of his seat with anger. "Guard, guard, get me out of here. Take me back to my cell," he says as he walks through the visiting room and out the door, going back to his cell.

Deacon Brown stands up and is watching him go out. "Son, son! Jayvorn, come back, let's just talk," he calls out to him as his eyes start to get teary. At that time another inmate who was with his wife, stands up and looks at Deacon Brown.

"Look Deacon, don't worry about it. He's just a lost, scared and angry boy right now. But God will see him through all this, so don't stop praying for him. I will keep an eye out for him," the other inmate says to Deacon Brown, as he shakes his hand and pats him on the arm.

"God bless you sir," Deacon Brown tells him.

"Thank you and God bless you," the inmate tells him as Deacon Brown turns and starts to walk out.

Keeping Family Close

As the years go by, Jayrode is in school practicing with his teammates. They are doing drill and learning how to work together as a team.

While Jayvorn is in the gym at the jail playing ball with his friends he met there.

Jayrode is in classes studying and trying to keep it all together while Jayvorn is at the jail school studying to get his GED.

Jayrode is out trying to find a job for the summer and trying to send money home to Tiff and their baby.

During this time Jayvorn is in the kitchen working on line in the jail.

As days go by Tiffany and the baby come up to see Jayrode on campus for the weekend.

As Edd and Clara comes to see Jayvorn in jail. He is shocked to see that they brought Tracy. He has a real good visit with them.

Jayrode is home for spring break. He is spending time with his mom , Tiff and the baby. He is shocked to see his son is walking and so big.

Jayvorn is in his cell writing a letter to Tracy as he is smiling at a picture of her he just got in the mail.

Jayrode is back in school and his team has just made it to the playoffs. They do lose in the first round, not before Jayrode finally got some play time in. He scored 18 points. As Jayvorn is in the TV room in the jail , he is watching the playoffs and sees his boy Jayrode playing on TV for the first time. Jayvorn gets happy as he starts to brag and tells everyone in the TV room that that is his boy and how they used to play together.

Four years later Cindy has moved to Pennsylvania to be closer to Jayrode. Tiffany is at her house for the weekend to visit Jayrode. She has come to see Ms. Spencer's new house as well.

"Ms. Spencer, I'm so glad you moved out here. It makes it so much easier for me and junior to see Jayrode, because when we would come up on the weekend, we would have to stay in hotels or at that dorm. That's no place for a baby," Tiffany tells her as they are sitting in the living room of Cindy's new house. Junior is running around playing with his toys.

"Yeah girl, I know because I been at his dorm and yes, I did get tired of spending all that money on hotels, every time I got to missing my baby boy," Cindy tells her as they are eating and watching Junior play.

"You know Ms. Spencer I really do love this place," she tells her as she looks out the window at the front yard. They look around the house and admire it all from where they are sitting. "You know what girl? I do to. It's sure better than that small apartment in the projects," Cindy tells her, smiling and feeling proud of where she lives, as she looks around kind of showing off.

"Yeah, but you did good raising Jayrode in the projects, by yourself didn't you?" Tiffany asks her as if she had something on her mind.

"Yeah, I did and I'm not knocking the projects, but this is a whole lot better. Why are you asking girl?" Cindy asks her as she looks at Tiffany's face and Cindy can tell she is hiding something or got something on her mind that she wanted to tell her.

"Oh it's nothing," Tiffany says to her in a soft and shy voice, with a sad face, trying to lie and hold back.

"Out with it girl? I'm a mother. I know when our kids are lying!" Cindy says to her with a real serious voice and that mother-look on her face.

"It's just I can't wait to get my own place because my parents are always riding me about the baby, me coming out here all the time and why Jayrode can't take the baby sometimes or spend more time with the baby so I can get a full-time job or go back to school. They are always trying to make it seem like Jayrode is not a part of Junior's life. That's why I put my application in for the projects. I hope they call me soon," Tiffany tells her as if she was relieved to get that off her chest.

"The projects! No, not my grandbaby. He's not being raised in any projects," Cindy tells her in a smart voice, as she reaches for Junior and picks him up and puts him on her lap. "And besides girl, it will take you forever to get in the projects in New York."

"I know, but with Jayrode having another year to go in college, by that time Junior will be five, going on six years old. I don't know what to do," Tiffany says as she shakes her head and looks at Cindy and Junior with a straight face.

"Well I do! You can just stay out here with me, and then I can keep my grandbaby. Then you can do what you need to do," Cindy tells her as she is playing with Junior on her lap.

"Are you sure Ms. Cindy?" Tiffany asks with her eyes wide open with a surprised and shocked look on her face as she starts to get all happy.

"I wouldn't have said it if I didn't mean it," Cindy tells her as she is still playing with junior.

"Thank you! Thank you! Thank you! You are a God sent," Tiffany tells her as she jumps up and gives Cindy a big hug and kiss on the cheek.

At that time Jayrode comes in the front door. He looks at his mom and Tiff.

"Hey mom!" he says as he walks over to them. "Are you about ready Tiff? Because I can drop you off at the bus station on my way to the game," he lets Tiffany know as he stands there waiting for her to get her stuff together.

"No! I'm not going anywhere. Your mother just said we can stay out here with her and move in. So when you get back from the game we can go to get Junior and my things from my house," she tells him with a big smile on her face as she is so happy to be moving close to him.

"Are you for real mom?" he asks his mom with a surprised look on his face as he turns to his mom. She is going towards the back door with Junior.

"Yeah, I told her it's ok. But that don't mean

there's going to be baby making going on up in my house. You got one and that's enough," she tells them as she goes out the back door with Junior, so he can play in the back yard while the sun was still out.

"Ah man, that's great Tiff," he tells her as he gives her a kiss, then heads back out the front door to go to his basketball game.

A year later Jayrode is in his senior year in college. It is basketball season and Jayvorn is in the TV room watching Sports Center as he usually does around this time of year, since he seen his best friend play in the playoffs on TV for the first time.

"Well it's the sweet sixteen, and we have a lot of hard playing, good teams this year," comes from the TV, one of the sportscaster says.

"Yeah we do, but the real story this year is about the Cinderella team from Penn State, Steve," the other sportscaster says

"You're right Pat. Penn State has wowed everyone by making it this far with the hard work from their star player Jayrode Spencer. I think they might be a sure in to win," Steve says.

"Well Steve, I might have to agree with you on that one. Even though he hasn't seen any game time in his freshman year and very little in his sophomore and junior years. He is now a senior and he is exploding all over the court. He is dominating the backboards as well. He can shoot just about anywhere on the floor and Steve, he is not afraid to pass the ball, so it's like there's no stopping this young man," Pat says.

"Well Pat, you know, it's just like the high school playoffs. If you can remember he shocked everyone by dominating the game and taking home the championship back then," Steve tells him.

"You're right, that is the first time we seen this young man and he took over and dominated every game, putting up higher and higher numbers each time he played," Pat tells him.

"Now do you believe me when I said he will be in the NBA someday?" Steve asks him.

"Yeah I do! But we first have to see if he can do what he did in high school now on the college level. With the way he is playing it doesn't seem to be too hard for this young man," Pat replies.

"Yeah, well just remember, when he get there I said it first," Steve says as they start to laugh.

"Yeah you said it, and we seen it," Pat says as he starts to laugh with him.

As Jayvorn is listening and watching everything they are saying, he starts to brag and cheer his boy on to everyone in the TV room.

"Yeah! Yeah! That's my boy. I told you my boy is going to take it all. That's why my boy is going to the NBA. See that's what I'm talking about. Two to the right baby! Two to the right, that's my boy," he says all excited.

As the game gets underway and narrows down to the Elite Eight, Penn State makes it with Jayrode scoring thirty-six points in the first game and winning it. He takes them on through scoring higher and higher numbers in each game. Winning them all for Penn State and taking them throw to the Final Four. Game scores of 108 to 86 and 126 to 101 with Jayrode scoring fifty-six points and up dominating all of the Elite Eight. In the Final Four Jayrode explodes really showing his stuff by scoring seventy-eight points and the game winning score of 154 to 110. Winning the Final Four taking Penn State to the Championship game. In the Championship game Jayrode takes over and puts up 86 points and 22 assists, with the game winning score of 172 to 98 blowing them out.

Jayvorn watches every game and gets more and more proud and excited for his boy and can't stop bragging and wondering what team his boy is going to play for at the NBA draft.

A few months later Jayvorn is in the TV room as the draft gets underway. Everyone is watching to see where Jayvorn's boy is going. After the first three rounds, Jayvorn is still waiting and watching closely at the TV hoping to see his boy.

"As the Suns next pick in the 4th round choice is Jayrode Spencer," the N.B.A. Commissioner says as Jayvorn gets all happy, jumping out of his seat. "Yeah, yeah, yeah! That's my boy," he said bragging to everyone in the TV room as he points to the TV and sees Jayrode standing next to the Suns manager, the NBA Commissioner and all the others. He looks and sees Tiffany is right by Jayrode's side. Jayvorn sees them, gets real quiet and looks at the TV real hard and funny.

"Yo, wait a minute! I know that girl! What

the fuck, that's my ex," he says as he is shocked to see Tiff and Jayrode together.

"Oh shit, that's fuck up!" an inmate says who is sitting behind him in the TV room.

"What you said?" Jayvorn asks him as he turns around and looks at him.

"I'm saying your boy stole your career and stole your girl. It wouldn't be surprising if he didn't set you up and that's why you're in here," the guy tells him.

"Oh shit! Oh man! Yo, that's fucked up! Yeah, that's messed up yo!" some of the other inmates start to say out loud.

"Man, you need to shut the fuck up and mind your business," he tells the guy with an attitude.

"Look man, no need to get mad at me. I'm not the one who took your spotlight and now fucking your girl," the guy tells Jayvorn out loud.

"Oh shit, you going to take that! That's fucked up yo! Yeah man, I know you not going to let him say that to you!" some of the other inmates say as they ride Jayvorn and egg him on, as some of them start to laugh at him messing with his ego.

"What!" Jayvorn shouts as he jumps up and punches the guy in the face, then takes his chair and hits him with it. As they start a big fight in the TV room, the guards rush in breaking them up and taking Jayvorn to the hole.

Six months later: Jayvorn is out of the hole. He is outside by himself on the basketball court playing ball and practicing, as he takes the ball and slams his hand on it and looks up at the sky.

"Every Saturday, every Wednesday, no matter what. That's what we said. So it's Wednesday. I'm here, where are you, or is that why you left me for dead?" he shouts as tears start to come from his eyes, as he drops on his knees and holds his head down on the basketball.

Moving up Again

Eight years later: Coach Davis is in his office at Fordham University. He is on his way out when his phone rings.

"Hello," Coach Davis says as he answers the phone.

"Hey Carl, this is James Wilson of the New York Knicks."

"Yeah, ok, how you doing," Carl says as he is kind of confused at why he was calling him.

"I'm doing great, but this call is about how you are doing," he tells Carl.

"Well, I'm doing pretty good and...." Carl says.

"Pretty good! The way we hear it, you're doing better than good," Mr. Wilson tells him.

"Ok, yeah what are you getting at?" Carl asks him, as to say I know you didn't call to talk about my health.

"Well, let me cut straight through the chase. We at the Knicks have been looking at all what you done with Fordham University over the last 14 to 15 years. I'm amazed to say we love what you have done by taking a non-elite lesser-known basketball school to the Final Four. Not once, not just twice, but three times and on the fourth time you won it all. Man we love to hear things like that," Mr. Wilson tells him.

"Well, I didn't do it by myself. I had a good staff and a great group of guys out there doing their thing too," Carl tells him.

"I know that, and you don't have to be so modest with me. I know with your leadership it took them most of the way," Mr. Wilson tells Carl.

"Yeah well, for me to lead, they had to listen and follow," Carl tells him.

"Well you are right about that. So that's why we here at the New York Knicks organization would like to know if you wouldn't mind jumping on board and leading us to some of those victories," Mr. Wilson asks him in a real excited voice.

"What? Are you for real, you're joking right?" Carl asks him happy but shocked.

"No I'm not joking; I'm for real about that. So how about it?" Mr. Wilson asks Carl.

"Well, yeah, cool! Great! I'm all for it," Carl tells him.

"Ok then, I guess I will take that as a yes. So I will see you when you get some time to come down to the organization, so we can get everything worked out, and get you familiar with the franchise," Mr. Wilson tells Carl.

"Well, how about tomorrow morning?" Carl asks him.

"Ok, great, see you tomorrow!" he tells Carl.

"Ok, thank you!" Carl says as he hangs up the phone all excited. "Yes!" Carl shouts as he kicks up one knee and clutches his fist and shoves his arm down by his side as to say, "I scored one!"

Seeing, Believing

A few months later Jayvorn is in the TV room watching Sports Center. He is seeing how the new basketball season is going to start, who is going to be on what team for the year as he watches and listens to the sportscaster.

"We are here at the New York Knicks conference room where the Knicks newly just signed head coach Carl Davis has just signed Jayrode Spencer to a new 6-year contract for 40 million dollars." comes from the TV. As the press conference gets underway Jayvorn starts to get upset as he sees Coach Davis and Jayrode sitting together at the table all happy and smiling.

"So Coach Davis how does it feel to be running the reigns of a pro ball team?" one of the sportscasters asks him.

"Well, I guess it will be like running any other team, as long as the guys work with me I will work with them," he answers.

"So what do you think you can do for the New York Knick to help them get back on a winning spree?" another reporter asks him.

"Well I guess by signing Jayrode here, who is an eight-year veteran and some of our new guys, we will mix things up and let our skill, talent and experience work everything out to a championship ring," Coach Davis says to them as he pats Jayrode on the back.

"So Jayrode, I seen you play here at the Garden in your senior year of high school. You exploded out there on the floor, shocking everyone for the first time, outscoring everyone with your high numbers and dominating every team. Do you think coming back now to the Garden after 15 plus years you can do it again?" Pat asks Jayrode.

"Well, this is about where I got my career off and running. When I walk out on that floor back then, for the first time, I was amazed. Right then I knew this is where I wanted to be, so now when I go out there I am going to do everything I need to do to get a win," Jayrode answers pat.

As Jayvorn is watching and listening to everything Jayrode is saying. He gets up out of his seat and walks over to the TV.

"Do you believe this shit? This guy takes my girl, my career, my life and now he's with my coach. Man I'm not watching this shit no more," Jayvorn says as he pushes the TV off the stand and knocks it to the floor blowing it out.

"Yo man! What the fuck! Are you fucking crazy? What the fuck is your problem?" everyone in the TV room starts saying as they jump up mad, angry and ready to fight. The guards rush in and take Jayvorn to the hole.

A few days later, Jayrode is at practice in the Knicks gym where he goes up to Coach Davis.

"Hey Coach! What's up? Do you know of any good high schools?" Jayrode asks.

"Yes, son I do," Coach Davis says.

"He will be a freshman this year. You know I just don't want him going to none of the schools I went to," Jayrode asks him as he is confiding in

140

Coach Davis.

"Well look Jayrode, I do know of one. Yes, let me make some calls and I will see what I can do" Coach Davis tells him.

"Ok let me know as soon as you can." Jayrode says as he runs off back into the layup line.

Second Offering

Later that night Jayvorn is in the hole, laying on his bed as he is talking to himself, replaying everything that went wrong in his life from the time of that dreadful day, the day he got on that bus.

"Man, oh man! I know, I know, I know I never had any drugs in my bag. The only time I put my bag down was in the park. The other time was that lady. Yeah! But she couldn't have put anything in my bag because she didn't have my bag long enough. So it had to have been Jayrode. He had to have something to do with this. But what? What is it God? What are you trying to tell me? Why did you do this to my life?" What did I do wrong for you to destroy my life like this?" he says to himself loudly as he becomes more mad, not knowing that an older inmate was standing there outside of his cell listening to him. It is the same guy from the visiting room who had talked with Deacon Brown.

"Hold on now son, is that why you so mad?" he asks Jayvorn looking at him from the other side of the bars.

"Look old school, you don't know anything about me or what I'm mad at!" Jayvorn tells him in an angry voice.

"You right. I don't. So let me ask you this, who are you mad at? Are you mad at God or are you mad at yourself?" he asks him.

"What! I'm mad at God because if he was real or if He was there for me, I wouldn't have gone through all this," Jayvorn tells him, as he is still angry.

"Look son, you need a lot of prayer and forgiveness in your life because you are very bitter and angry at the wrong person," he tells Jayvorn.

"Look old school, you can go ahead with all that, because I did all my praying when I came in and forgiveness, please, what do I need forgiveness for, I didn't do anything to God," Jayvorn tells him as he looks up at him from his bed. The old man shakes his head and looks back at Jayvorn.

"I got something for you," he tells Jayvorn as he reaches into his back pocket and pulls out a pocket Bible.

"Man please, what's that?" Jayvorn asks him as he sits up on his bed.

"Look, I just want you to read it," he says to Jayvorn as he hands it to him.

"I read it already. Ain't nothing in there but a bunch of words," Jayvorn tells him as he takes the Bible and tosses it on his desk.

"Yeah, but those words have everything you need and you can find your peace," he tells Jayvorn.

"Please, what I need, it's not in there," Jayvorn says as he lies back down on his bed. The man just looks at Jayvorn for a little bit and shakes his head, then walks off.

The Beginning of a Second Change

As the season gets underway; Jayrode is exploding as he and his newfound team, the New York Knicks go on a winning spree.

While Junior is getting used to his new school and does not like it at all.

The Knicks are on the road, Jayrode is blowing teams away as he brings the Knicks closer to a championship.

Junior on the other hand has found a new place where he can hid and get away from everyone and everything on the bleachers in the back of the soccer fields.

The Knicks are at home and just have won the last game that puts them I the playoffs. All the sports announcers are saying how they are sure to win the Eastern Conference with home court advantage.

Junior is in class working on a class project by himself as everyone is paired up working as teams.

Jayrode is at the gym. He is warming up getting ready to practice with his team for the big game in a few days.

Junior is hanging out at his new spot, the bleachers as he is waiting for his mom to come get him, as he would do every day.

The Big Game

At the Garden days later, as you see the two sports announcers, Steve and Pat with the Knicks and Jayrode as they are warming up on the floor.

"It's game time here at the Garden, on a wild and crazy Friday," Steve says.

"Yes, it is Steve. The New York Knicks are about to play the first game of the playoff and who would have thought they would have made it all the way to the Big Show," Pat says.

"Well, let's not forget who helped them get here Pat," Steve says.

"Oh you know I can't Jayrode has been awesome, just blowing the competition away," Pat says.

"Yes he has. Even though the Knicks had some rough spots in the beginning, Jayrode always seem to pull them back together and come through with a win," Steve says.

"Yes you are right about that now Steve. But we will have to see what they do against the number one ranking team, the Chicago Bulls. The Bulls will hold on and take them all the way to game 7," Pat says to Steve.

"And you know what Pat; the way these teams are playing it just might go that far. Because it is said win or go home and neither one of these teams wants to go home," Steve says. As the Knicks warming up behind them for the big game tonight.

Around the same time back at the school

Junior is getting out of school for the day. He is heading for the bleachers as he would always do to wait for his mom to come pick him up. At that time there are three boys under the bleachers playing and messing around.

"Come on man, let me see it," one of the boys says to the boy with a black bookbag on his back.

"I don't know man; I don't want to get in trouble. What if someone else sees it?" the one with the book bag says.

As Junior is coming out of the school he is walking through the field. He checks his watch to see what time it is. As he listens to his Walkman, he heads to his spot on the bleachers.

"Man, its 4:35pm. Now and my dad's game starts at 7pm., so that gives mom one hour to come get me and we have 1 1/2 hours to get to dad's game," he says to himself.

"Come on man, I told you he don't have one, he's just lying," the other boy says to the first boy, talking about the boy with the black bag.

"Yeah man, I think you're right. He's a liar. He doesn't have one," the first boy says to his friend talking about the one with the bag.

"What! You're talking about I'm not a liar. I do have it right in my bag. See!" The boy with the bag says as he reaches in his bag and pulls it out.

As Junior is at the bottom of the bleachers he is fixing his Walkman. He does not notice the three boys under the bleachers or hear them.

"See man, look! I told you," the boy with

the bag says as he shows the two boys a black gun.

"Oh man, let me check it out," the first boy asks as he goes to reach for the gun.

"Man, is it real?" the other boy asks as he goes to reach for it as well.

"Yeah man, it's real," the boy with the bag says as he hands it to them.

As Junior is about to go up the stairs of the bleachers, he hears a bang ring out. He jumps from the loud sound, as he looks around and starts to go behind the bleachers to hide and duck. At the same time the two boys run out from behind the bleachers. As they are running out, one of the boys bumps into Junior, knocking him down. As Junior get up he looks and see a boy lying on the ground as the other two boys runs off. Junior walks under the bleachers and kicks the gun that the boy dropped when he bumped into Junior. As junior looks down and sees the gun, he bends down and picks it up and starts to walk over to the boy on the ground. As he gets over to the boy he sees the boy is lying next to a black bag and is on the ground kicking and gasping. Junior bends down to see if he's ok. He touches his chest to see if he is breathing and checking him out. Junior touches the boy and gets his blood on his hands. At that time Junior looks up and sees a whole crowd of people crowding around the outside of the bleachers looking at him. As he stands up Junior doesn't know that he still has the gun in his hand. "Drop it son, drop it," the school security guard yells to Junior. As Junior looks at his hand and sees he still has the gun in his hand, he

147

drops it and the security guard rushes him.

"Oh my God, look, he shot that boy! He shot him, he shot him!" comes from the crowd of people standing around.

"What! I didn't do it. It wasn't me, it was two other boys," Junior says out loud. As he looks around in the crowd to see if he can see the two boys. While the guards put Junior in handcuffs and calls for the police and the ambulance for the boy on the ground on their radio.

Two and a half hours later: back at the Garden. As the game gets started, Jayrode is on the court playing at his best.

At that time the police are at the scene questioning Junior and everyone there. As the ambulance is rushing the boy off to the hospital, Tiffany pulls up to get Junior. She looks around to see all the commotion of the police and everything. She looks around looking for Junior because she is late for picking him up.

As Jayrode looks to be at the top of his game, he's outscoring the Bulls in the beginning of the first half.

Tiffany starts to go off. As she spots Junior in the back of a police car handcuffed, she is trying to find out why they have her son, and what is going on. By the time she finds out and gets someone to talk to her and she is going off on everyone. Tiffany is getting more and more upset and mad as she can't get Jayrode on the phone.

By the end of the first half, the game is tied up as Jayrode and the Knicks go into the locker room for halftime.

Tiffany is trying to call Jayrode over and over again on his cell phone. She gets no answer. The police start to take Junior down to the station in the police car.

Jayrode heads back out to the floor to start the second half of the game, as the Knicks are all hyped up.

Tiffany is at the precinct where they have Junior. She is still trying to get in touch with Jayrode as his cell phone is off in his bag. Tiffany finally calls the locker room of the Knicks. As the phone rings for a long time, she is about to hang up when she gets someone.

"Hello, Knicks locker room," one of the staff members says as he answers the phone.

"Yes! This is Tiffany Spencer. I need to talk to my husband Jayrode," she said all hyped, mad and panicky. As she is confused and upset of what is going on. She doesn't know what to do.

"I'm sorry, but the team is back on the floor for the second half of the game," he tells her.

"What! Screw that fucking game. You get my husband on the phone right now!" she tells him real mad and nasty, as she is pissed off that she couldn't get him on his cell phone and he is playing a basketball game while his son is going to jail.

"I'm sorry! Please calm down Mrs. Spencer. What I can do is take a message and have him call you right back ASAP," the guy tells her.

"Yeah, well you tell him I need him right now. His son just got arrested at school, so he needs to be here with me and not at no game," Tiffany tells him all upset.

"Ok Mrs. Spencer, I will get this right out to him, right now," he tells her as he hangs up the phone, and writes on a piece of paper: Jayrode call your wife, your son got arrested at school, and goes out to the floor where Jayrode is on the court playing. As it is getting close to the end of the second half and the Bulls are up by four points, the guy hands the paper to the assistant coach. He tells him to make sure you give this to Jayrode when he gets off the court. As Jayrode hit a 3-pointer, the Bulls are up by one. They are all over Jayrode as the time gets down to the wire. The Assistant Coach takes the paper and clips it on the coach's clipboard, with the note on the other side. As Coach Davis calls for a time out with less than two minutes to go in the game, the Bulls are up by one point. Coach Davis grabs the clipboard to try to make some kind of play to free up a shot.

"Look Coach, I got just the play," Jayrode says as he takes the clipboard and starts to write on the back of the note. He is drawing out a play.

"It goes like this, I come down with the ball when I get to the top of the key, I fake once to the right, then again to the right, and you!" he says as he points to one of his teammates, "be on my right as I break to my left. I will shoot the ball back to you that leaves you open to take the shot or put it up for the alley-oop!" he tells them.

"Look Coach, this is a play me and my boy used to do back in high school. It's called Two to

150

the Right!" Jayrode says as he passes the clipboard back to Coach Davis.

"Ok go with it," Coach Davis says as he looks at the play as if he has seen it somewhere before. He sends the team back on the floor. As Jayrode sets up for the play the ball is pass in to Jayrode and he come down court to the top of the key and starts it off. Once, then twice to the right and then he breaks left and passes it off to his teammate and runs down for the alley-oop. As the clock runs down the ball is up and right there at Jayrode hands Slam! Two points, Jayrode pulls it off and win it for the Knicks, by one point. The crowd goes wild. Jayrode jumps up and down as his team lifts him in the air. He yells "Two to the right baby, two to the right!" as he points at Coach Davis. Coach Davis looks at him and thinks as he says to himself "Where did I see this play, I know I seen this play before," as Jayrode starts to look around for his wife and son, who he doesn't see anywhere in sight. As he makes it back to the locker room to get to his cell phone in his bag to call his wife.

"Hey Tiff, what's up baby we won! Where are you and Junior? I look all around this place and I did not see you two all game." he asks her as she answers the phone. He is looking for them as he doesn't know all that happened to Junior at his school.

"What! Of course you didn't see us. I'm down here at the precinct with your son, who has just been arrested for supposedly shooting some boy in his school! You need to be getting down here," she tells him all mad, hostile and hysterical.

"What! What are you talking about?" he asks her puzzled and shocked.

"If you would have answered your phone and not been all into that game you would know what I'm talking about," she tells him all mad and frantic.

"Look, I'm on my way. Just tell me where you are," he asks her as he grabs his bag and run out the locker room through the crowd and heads out the Garden. As Coach Davis looks up at Jayrode as he runs out. He starts to wonder where he is going.

Things Start to Come Out

Later that night, Coach Davis is at his house in his study room. He is looking at the play Jayrode wrote down, the one that just won them the first game.

"I know I seen this play before, but where?" he asks himself. As he starts to think and picks up the paper and looks at it, he sees that there is some writing on the other side. He turns it over and sees what it says. In shock he picks up his desk phone and makes a call.

"Hello," a person says on the other end of the phone.

"Hey Paul, I'm sorry to be calling you so late," Coach Davis says.

"It's ok Carl, I was not asleep," Paul says.

"Well, I'm calling to try to find out what's going on. I got this little note here that says Jayrode's son has just been arrested at school."

"Yeah, that's why I'm still up. It's been hard trying to get the school out of this one Carl," Paul tells him, as if he was trying to insinuate something.

"What Paul? What are you saying?" Carl asks him in a confusing voice.

"Look Carl, you are a good friend and colleague, but we don't need you sending us anymore kids that are going to embarrass our school."

"What did you say Paul?" Carl asks him, now getting upset.

"Look Carl, why don't you talk to this kid's

153

father, because he is saying the same thing the last one did: It's not me, I didn't do it and he claims it was someone else," Paul tells him in a smart voice.

"You know what Paul, I'm really sorry I called you," Carl tells him as he hangs up the phone in his ear.

Carl sits back in chair, shaking his head and looking around; he can't believe what just happened. He sees a box in his closet the one from his old high school that has all his stuff in it. He goes to get it and puts it on his desk, looking through it for the first time since he packed it. He sees the old itinerary from the last game that Jayvorn was to play in. It has the entire team's name on it. He notices something on the back. He turns it over and sees, "Jayrode Spencer, 755 E. 166 St., (718) 328-8999." As Coach Davis drops his head and tears fall from his eyes.

At the same time all this going on, a corrections officer walks Junior down a cell block very slowly, wearing an orange jumpsuit, holding a bed roll and a brown bag. They get to an open cell. Junior looks inside and sees a sink, toilet, desk, and a bed with the mat folded up. He steps inside as the correction officer walks off. "Boom!" the door shuts behind him, he jumps, looks around at the cell and his eyes start to tear up. He puts the bag down on the desk and unfolds the mat.

He sees a Bible laying there as if someone left it for him he puts the bed roll-down on the bed, picks up the Bible, and drops to his knees and closes his eyes to pray. "Lord, what have I done?

How did I get here? What did I do? Help me Jesus. I need you now more than ever! Please God get me out of this trouble."

He opens his eyes, looks up and sees Jayvorn's name on the wall, where he wrote: "God bless me, protect me. Take me out of this place, Jayvorn Hall." Then Junior drops his head and tears falls from his eyes.

The next day, Coach Davis is in his office at the Knicks gym. Jayrode comes in to his office to talk with him.

"Hey Coach, can I talk with you?" Jayrode asks him as he steps in and closes the door.

"Yes Jayrode. I need to talk to you as well," Carl tells him as Jayrode starts to take a seat.

"Look Coach, I'm not going to be able to play, my son got arrested last night and I need to be there for my family," he tells him.

"I know. I made a few calls and tried to find out something about it," Coach Davis tells him.

"Oh yeah! What did you find out Coach?" Jayrode asks him as he stands up kind of excited.

"Not very much," he says. "But I did find out one thing." Coach Davis tells him as he looks up at him.

"Yeah, what's that?" Jayrode asks.

"That we have the same old friend."

"Ok, who's that?"

"Karma! Do you know about Karma?" Carl asks him.

"What Karma! Come on Coach, what that got to do with my son?" Jayrode ask him as he starts to look

155

puzzled and trying to find out what Coach Davis was trying to say.

"Karma. It's like this- When you do something good something good happens," Coach Davis starts to explain to him as he reaches on his desk and passes Jayrode a paper. "And When you do something bad, something bad happens." Coach Davis tells him as Jayrode looks at it and sees his name and old address on it. Then, Jayrode turns the paper over and sees a bunch of names on it. It says itinerary on top and at the bottom of the names is Jayvorn Hall. Jayrode drops his head as he sees his best friend's name on it.

"So Coach, what are you telling me?" Jayrode asks him as he can't believe he is the same Coach that helped Jayvorn out back in high school.

"Well, what I am saying is, on that day when our friend got arrested, he was telling me about a friend who could have probably helped him out, but I didn't believe him. And you know what, he believed in you so much that before that day he came to me bragging and telling me all about you and trying to get you on his team back in high school."

"So Coach, what do I got to do about this?" Jayrode asks him as he starts to think of all that happening and how he was not there for his friend.

"Now what you got to do? I don't know that, and can't tell you, but what you need to do is get things right," Coach Davis tells him as he walks over and puts his hand on his shoulder, then walks out of the office, leaving Jayrode there.

Jayrode drops his head and starts to cry.

Finding Themselves

Jayrode is driving around thinking and talking to himself. "I can't believe this. No! No! Not now. I'm at the highlight of my life, the top of my game. And why my son, what do he have to do with all this!"

He pulls up in front of a church. It is the church he used to go to when he was a kid in high school, without knowing where he was going or why he was led there. He looks out his car window and sees it is still open.

Later that night, Jayvorn is in his cell in the hole. He is laying down trying to sleep. He tosses and turns as if something was bothering him and he could not get any rest. He looks over at the desk and sees the little pocket Bible. He reaches for it and gets out of bed, just drops to his knees and starts to pray: "Forgive me Lord…"

He turns his car around and parks. He goes into the church. When he gets inside he sees no one is inside. As he goes up to the altar, he drops on his knees and starts to pray:

"Forgive me Lord, I'm sorry for not believing in you. Lord Jesus, just tell me what to do. I need you Jesus, I believe in you Jesus, forgive me Lord God, just tell me what I need to do to make it all right, please Jesus forgive me. I do accept you in my heart, help me through this one for I don't know what to do!" They both say as they drop their heads and start to cry. As Jayrode is on his knees he doesn't notice Deacon Brown off standing to the side.

Deacon Brown walks over to see who it is. . Jayrode is crying on his knees. "Jayrode, son is that you? as he gets closer to see if it is him. .

"I'm sorry Coach Brown, I know I was wrong. I know I should have been there for him. I was young and scared. It's my fault. I should have told someone, I should have helped him out, he was my best friend, my brother, all I had," Jayrode says as he stands and turns to Deacon Brown and cries on his shoulder as a son would do with his father.

"Well son, you know what you need to do to get them demons off your back, and get things right," Deacon Brown tells him as he holds Jayrode in his arms and consoles with him.

"Yes! Yes! I do and first thing in the morning I will get it right, I promise, I will take care of everything and set it straight no matter what," Jayrode says as he is standing at the altar with Deacon Brown.

Returning Lives

The very next morning, Jayrode is at his son's lawyer's office. As he walks into her office, she starts to pull out everything she was working on in his son's case.

"Hello, Mr. Spencer, how are you to day?" his son's lawyer asks him as he walks into her office, and she get the papers ready for him.

"Hello Mrs. Yvette," he replies as he takes a seat at her desk.

"Look Mr. Spencer, I have to be straight with you. It doesn't look so good for your son right now. But you pay for the best and I'm the best. So I want you to know I will fight very hard to get your son off," Mrs. Yvette tells him, as she looks at him as if he looks worried.

"Thank you very much," Jayrode tells her as he sits there looking worried, confused and scared, as he thinks to himself. ("Not only do I have to get my son out of this trouble, I have to get my best friend out of trouble, as well.")

"Here it is Mr. Spencer. All it seems to me is they have nothing to go on. As for now, they have just some statements of people seeing your son after the shot was fired so it looks like no one really saw your son firing the shot. But here's where it gets messy. They have your son standing over the boy with the gun in his hands. It looks like; yes they found some gunpowder on your son's shorts and the boy's blood, which was on his hand as well. So I do have a lot of work in front of me, but your son

160

stated that he did not do it. There were two other boys who had to have shoot him. The two boys who ran out from under the bleachers. So I will have my investigator out looking for these two boys. Now here comes some more bad or good news. I have to tell you, as it seems, the boy is in the hospital. He is in a coma and can't speak. It is touch and go for him as of now. So as soon as there is any word on his condition I will let you know, good or bad. If the boy makes it, we will be able to talk to him and clear all this up. But if he don't, I have to let you know this, if he dies, they will be back out to charge your son with manslaughter. So I don't want you to be caught off guard if this does happen. I will be preparing for that as well," she tells Jayrode as he still looks stressed.

"That's good, that's real good. I know you got everything under control for my son," he tells her as he looks at her with a look of relief and stress on his face, as if he can't believe all this is happening to him all at once. "But I need to talk to you about another case," he tells her as he shakes his head and looks at her and she sits back in her chair and looks at him.

"I'm listening," she says to him.

"Well, years ago, I saw a guy I know shoot a cop. Even though I didn't do nothing I was involved because at that time I was holding, or should I say carrying, things for him I should not have had. But the real case is my friend, my best friend, went to jail because of what I was doing. So I need to make it right, no matter what I need to do this. I need to

161

help him out," he tells her.

"Well Mr. Spencer, there is nothing I can do for your friend as for now. I mean how long has it been?" she asks him.

"Well it's been over 15 years now."

"Well there it is, Mr. Spencer. A case that old, the courts may not have any records of it, or it might be closed unless your friend went to trial and there is or he has some kind of appeal going on. Besides, Mr. Spencer I don't know anything about your friend's case. So I don't think there is much I can do for him unless you tell me everything," she tells him as she looks at him.

Jayrode takes a deep breath and starts to tell his son lawyer everything that happened to him that night, then everything he knows about Jayvorn's case and that yes he knows Jayvorn went to trial. He tells her Jayvorn's lawyer name and everything that he got from Deacon Brown. As his son lawyer sits back in amazement of all that she just heard, she looks at Jayrode and shakes her head.

"Well let me see what I can do," she says as she gets on the phone and starts to make some calls.

"Hello Mr. Tanner," Yvette says as she finally gets Jayvorn's lawyer on the phone.

"Yes, may I ask who is calling?" Mr. Tanner asks her.

"Well, my name is Yvette Hall and I'm calling on behalf of my client, Jayrode Spencer and your client, Jayvorn Hall. No relation, I might add. Do you remember? It seems that my client, Mr. Spencer may have something that might help your client, Mr. Hall out with," she tells him.

"Yes, I think I do remember something about that. Yes my client, Mr. Hall mentioned a Jayrode, but I think, can you hold on for a minute while I get his case out? Yes, I think I do remember. Oh here it is, yes, Jayvorn asked me to talk to a Jayrode because he was one of the last persons who had been near his bag at the time. He said he would be able to tell me if he seen someone putting something in his bag or something in that manner," Mr. Tanner tells Mrs. Hall as she puts him on the speaker phone, so Jayrode can listen.

"No, no one put anything in his bag. He took my bag by accident, and I got his," Jayrode tells them both.

"That's great to hear now, but it would have been better to hear that, what, 16 years ago in trial. Now with no evidence that's going to be hard to prove it. A judge will just throw it out. I mean I could have used you on the witness stand when I had you on my witness list, but now a judge will say it sounds like a friend wants to just help another friend out and where or why he wasn't there back then," Mr. Tanner says on the phone.

"Yes, I understand and I told my client that, but I know there is something we can do," Yvette asks.

"Yeah! Yeah! What about the tape," Jayrode says all excited.

"Tape, what tape?" Mr. Tanner asks.

"Yes, what tape? You never told me about a tape. I think we need to talk again, can you hold on

163

Mr. Tanner." Yvette asks him as she puts him on hold. "Look Mr. Spencer I can't represent you if you don't tell me everything or you keep things from me. And please Mr. Spencer stop yelling out everything and let me do the talking so I can try to keep you out of some trouble or at least out of jail." Yvette tells him after she puts Mr. Tanner on hold.

"Ok Mrs. Hall I understand but I need to do what I need to do." Jayrode tells her.

"Ok Mr. Tanner we are back." Mrs. Hall says as she takes him off hold.

"Now what tape are you talking about?" Mr. Tanner asks.

"The cop! The cop Dee shot had a tape recorder on him and I know I had to say Jayvorn's name or something that can help him, because that's when I realized I had his bag and he had mine," Jayrode tells them.

"Well if there's a tape with all that, then I will make some calls to try to find or get it," Mr. Tanner says to them.

"Well if you have my client on your witness list, I will see what I can do to get your client back in court and then we will have to see what we have to do for my client. Then I will get back with you," Mrs. Hall tells him.

"And I will do the same. And when I get this tape I will make sure you are the first to hear it." Mr. Tanner tells her. As they hang up the phone, Jayrode looks at Mrs. Hall and she looks back at him and starts to shake her head as she tells him what he is looking at and what can come out of all this.

Confessions

A few weeks later: Jayrode is in the courtroom on the witness stand, looking at Jayvorn for the first time in over 16 years.

Jayvorn's lawyer questions him about the day at hand. "So Mr. Spencer, tell us what happened early that day in the park," Mr. Tanner asks him.

"Well, Jayvorn came into the park to tell me about he was going to a basketball game and how he was not going to be able to work out with me. When he left, he took my bag by accident and I got his. By the time I realized it, it was too late," Jayrode says.

"So when you say too late, you mean too late to get it back or too late for what?"

"Yes, to get it back."

"And when did you know that Mr. Hall had your bag and you had his?"

"When I was giving it to Dee, who at that time he had just shot a cop and was about to shoot me."

"So why are you here now? And why did you not come forth earlier? Or is this a why to just help your friend?"

"Because at that time I was afraid for my life and scared of what might happen to me if I went to the police," Jayrode tells the court.

"So why now tell this court all this. Are you not afraid of this Dee or going to jail?" he asks Jayrode.

"Well Dee got killed that day, and no, I want to tell the truth. I need to do the right thing and this is the right thing," Jayrode says.

"So why should we take your word for it? Why should we not just think you are telling us all this to help get a friend off the hook?" Mr. Tanner asks.

"Because when Dee shot that cop, the cop had a tape recorder on him."

Mr. Tanner holds up the silver tape recorder. "Your Honor, I would like to place this into evidence as exhibit D," Mr. Tanner asks the Judge.

"Do the people have any objections," the Judge asks the D.A.

"No, not at this time," the D.A. answers.

"So noted," the Judge says. "It is accepted."

"At this time I would like to play the tape, which has been in the police evidence room all this time," Mr. Tanner says as he places it down in front of Jayrode.

At that same time, Jayrode is on the witness stand the boy who was shot is in the hospital lying in a coma. His mother and father are in the room crying and praying over him. There is a policeman right outside his door. His mother sits by his side holding his hand with her head down and eyes closed. All of a sudden, the boy starts to move his fingers. Then he starts to gasp for air, he is waking up out of the coma and his mother jumps up as she fells his hand moving and hears him gasping for air. She looks up at his face and sees his eyes open.

"Oh my God! Nurse, nurse come quick. He's up! My son's up!" she shouts as she gets excited and her husband does as well. The nurses and doctors come running into the room.

"Calm down son, calm down," one of the doctors says, "So I can pull this out of your nose," he tells the boy as the nurses hold his mom and dad back.

"Mom! Mom! Mom, where am I? What happened?" the boy calls out to his mother.

"You're in the hospital. You got shot by that boy Jayrode, Junior," his mom tells him.

"What! He didn't shoot me!" the boy says as the cop is standing right next to the doctors, nurses and his mom and dad.

"What did you say son?" the cop asks him.

"He didn't shoot me. It was my two friends," the boy tells the cop as the cop writes everything down and calls the D.A. and his precinct.

Back at the trial, Mr. Tanner pushes the play button on the tape recorder.

"Yo, Jayrock, where the fuck have you been, you know you late."

"I'm sorry Dee. I just had to let my boy Jayvorn know that I was not going to make practice today."

"Yo, get the hell over here. I told you that damn basketball is going to get your ass in trouble someday. Now where's my shit?"

"I got it right here Dee."

"Oh shit! This is not my bag. This is

Jayvorn's bag. Yo, Dee I got to go catch him."

"What the fuck you mean. Where's my shit."

"Look Dee, my boy Jayvorn got my bag by accident and I got his. He just went to the bus depot to go to a basketball tournament. If I leave now I can probably catch him, or I can get it from him when he gets back."

"What?"

"It's a no go. It's a no go"

"What the fuck, what you mean it's a no go. What you trying to set me up?"

(Bang)

"You shot him Dee!"

"Shots fired! Shots fired!"

"Jump!"

"Now I'm going to kill this little motherfucker!"

Click. Mr. Tanner stops the tape.

"Now Mr. Spencer, is there anything else you would like to say at this time?" Mr. Tanner asks him.

"Yes! I just want to say: Two to the right baby boy, two to the right!" Jayrode says as he looks at Jayvorn shaking his head as tears start to fall from his eyes. Jayvorn looks at him and smiles as he nods his head and his eyes get watery.

Jayrode is standing in the hallway outside the court room with Tiffany, Junior and Yvette. As Yvette is telling him how well he did on the stand and what to look forward to for the D.A., a court bailiff steps out of the courtroom and hands her a paper. As she reads it and she smiles and looks at

Jayrode and his family.

"Well Mr. Spencer I got some good news. The boy is out of the coma and is doing ok," she tells them.

"That's great!" Tiffany says as she gets all happy.

"Thank you, Jesus!" Jayrode said as he gets all excited.

"That's not all; he told the police who shot him. So now the D.A. is going to drop all charges on your son," she let them know.

"Oh, thank you Jesus! Thank you, Jesus!" they all yell as they give each other a big hug.

"Now look, Mr. Spencer that good news for your son that he got off, but we still have to see and worry about what the D.A. is going to do with you," Yvette lets him know.

"Look, it doesn't matter what they do to me. My son is ok and I got everything straight with God. I got it right now!" Jayrode tells her.

Return to a Previous Life

A few months later: At the start of the next basketball season, at the opening, of the first game of the New York Knicks. As the team is being announced in the Garden, the team runs onto the court.

The announcer says: "Now starting at point guard from New York for the New York Knick, Number 22, Jay....vorn Hall," as Jayvorn runs out on the court giving everyone five. He looks over at his coach who is Coach Davis and put up two fingers and yells: Two to the right, coach, two to the right!" and points at him and Coach Davis points back at Jayvorn.

Jayvorn then looks up in the stands and he sees his mom, dad, and Tracy all clapping and cheering him on.

THE END

Made in the USA
Middletown, DE
05 September 2021